RUNNING BETWEEN TREES

a novel

GOGO C. OKEKE

Published by Golden Girl Press
Design and distribution by Bublish

ISBN: 978-1-647047-50-4 (paperback)
ISBN: 978-1-647047-52-8 (eBook)

To my son Mylo.
For being my reason for everything.
Including not publishing this book sooner.

PROLOGUE

The night is quiet except for the screams coming from right behind my head. I am lying on my belly with my arms locked around Dorcy's legs, flexing my muscles as hard as I can. He's on his back, writhing around on the complex's wet grass, screaming at the three of us as we hold him in a supine restraint. Derrick and Simone have his arms locked in. Propped up on my side, I strain my neck to avoid getting kicked in the face.

Dorcy is a thirteen-year-old autistic boy with a demure disposition, small but surprisingly athletic. I am on my twenty-fourth restraint since starting at this centre, and I still remember the first time I got pulled into one of these. I could not get out of bed the next day. The muscle aches that would subsequently accompany every one often left me wondering how horrible it must feel for the child being held down. Now a veteran of the maneuver, I can allow my mind to wander, to leave the chaos. My body has become accustomed to the pain, both physical and psychological.

Though I'm wearing only my work T-shirt and jeans, this deliciously warm December in Pittsburgh has kept us all from freezing out here on the wet grass.

Feels like it's been about twenty minutes, I think, praying Dorcy will de-escalate soon. *At least he's taking longer breaks between outbursts.*

"Aren't you tired, Dorcy?" I whisper. "I know I am." Simone purses her lips in a forced smile as our eyes meet, and her expression looks sad and tired. My colleagues have told me privately that they hate these restraints, as I do. It seems violent to use our bodies against these children.

Restraints are used only in response to aggressive behaviours, my supervisor had assured me when I expressed concern.

I twist my neck far away enough to look up at the night sky. A scattering of silent, celestial stars twinkles back at me, seeming to ask, "What are you doing?"

Sometimes I'm not sure, but it's for his safety and ours.

To think that just about an hour ago, we were all inside the common room watching Dorcy play with three other children who are younger than him. In what seemed like a flash, he went from mimicking train sounds to knocking down one of the other boys over a brief misunderstanding. The speed and ease with which all three of us scuttled the other kids to safety and ran after Dorcy as he stormed outside demonstrated just how precise and finely tuned our process has become. We knew the drill all too well.

A swift kick to my rib cage brings me back into the chaos. I shift from looking heavenward to face him, arms locking in tighter around his legs. I study his small frame. For a minute he stops struggling and looks at Derrick on the left. He starts to bang his head on the dirt ground, and the soft thud echoes through the crisp night air. Simone puts her hand under his head, and Dorcy immediately starts biting the skin off his hand. We all groan and look away so that we don't lose our grips in an attempt to stop him. If we let go of him, he'll do far more harm to himself.

"Calm down, buddy," I call to him, wondering if he had noticed the stars. Perhaps they could help him get out of this torture.

Watching him cry in physical and emotional pain, I realize how foolish it was to tell him to calm down. When he gets this escalated, he only wants everything around him to burn, himself especially, and if the stars managed to come down, they would have to burn as well. What trauma had fractured this boy's mind so much that he would immediately start to pound his fist into his own eye or bite the skin off his hands, not to mention bang that small head merci-lessly against the ground? My Nigerian brain would say the boy is clearly possessed by a particularly perverted marine spirit and that being this close to him is the one thing not to do. Of course, I know that's not the case. I can recite psychological theories that explain such self-harming behaviours in my sleep. Yet nothing in all of my schooling prepared me for the strangeness of actually watching a person impose such pain on himself.

This child needs to be home with his family. That's where he wants to be.

Maybe that's what he's thinking right now as his face shifts in anguish. Or maybe he isn't even thinking about any of this. Maybe his body is perpetually on autopilot to self-sabotage, as I have seen working with child victims of trauma. Unlike the other kids on the autism spectrum, Dorcy has embraced harm as a constant part of his existence, and so he must initiate it at all times, by proxy or by self. It suddenly dawns on me how ironic it is that he flinches from being held down and yet welcomes the pain of skinning himself.

Only trauma can do that to a person. I start to feel my arm go to sleep under the tight grip of his legs and move myself a little.

Oops, I just caught a serving of spit right in the eye, and I know it was meant for me.

What does that matter? The constellation of affairs on this par-ticular night is so horrific that being spat at seems like a welcome peace offering.

"All right, buddy, you're gonna be good?" I hear one of my col-leagues say to the boy, having negotiated that he is now calm and will be released.

We raise him up slowly, alert to any shift in behaviours which would signal the need for another restraint.

As we walk back into the building, rolling our necks and stretching our body parts, Bruno Mars sings "Marry You" mockingly in my head.

It's true what they say about adrenaline; I'm just now starting to feel my neck smarting from when he scratched my skin off.

Chapter 1

THE PRIVILEGED IMMIGRANT

I climbed to the fifth floor of the cathedral of learning, where Professor Bodorf's office was, panting from ascending the flights of stairs. I couldn't understand why people would take the elevator and miss the secret messages on the walls, like clues to a path.

Hufflepuff beware.

Mischief managed.

I reminisced about my school days when I scoffed at the writers, wondering if they put as much thought into their studies as they did into all their nonsense scribbles.

But I came to appreciate it as part of school tradition. I bounded up the stairs and couldn't resist taking a detour to the third floor. I walked through the corridor, looking for random flights of hidden stairs and pretending I didn't know where the spooky dome would lead. I busted out to the second floor with the twenty-eight nationality rooms that were a nod to cultures of which people hardly ever concerned themselves. I passed the lounge, where students noisily cackled away during study time. These kids still had no regard for decorum and history.

This was my alma mater, a place so inspiring of poetry and philosophy. I missed studying here. I took every opportunity to come back, and today my order of business was meeting the professor for our periodic check-ins per the mentoring program. He was my favourite instructor throughout my undergrad years, and I was glad that we'd been paired.

"Hello, sir." I walked into his Victorian-style office to see him with a newspaper in hand like a stereotypical old man from the movies. *Who still reads newspapers in 2011?*

"Good day, Samira. Give me one second." He put down the newspaper and clicked at his computer screen, his glasses almost falling off the bridge of his nose.

"Done!" he said, picking up his phone and wallet from the desk. As we walked out of the office, the secretary gave us both a nod. I smiled back, awkwardly shuffling through my handbag. I always wondered what the woman thought of me when I visited the professor. Whatever suspicions she had of the nature of our relationship would certainly fly, as the professor was too aloof to shut them down.

Perhaps I saw in the professor the things I loved about my father. He was, to me, a version of what Dahdee would have been had he stayed in Nigeria. Professor Bodorf was an unanimated older Black man with silvery white hair and big black facial moles. He taught developmental psychology, and although he laughed at times in his classes, he mostly had a serious way about him. He was impatient about any time wasting but approached us foreign students with curiosity, often inviting us to his home, where his wife would make yummy southern food.

We settled into a booth at the cafeteria on the ground floor, me with tea and some desserts while he had black coffee.

"How's it going at the centre?" he asked, taking a sip.

"Good. I'm learning so much about different diagnoses." I sighed. "It's just that these kids need so much help; it's really sad."

"What are some of the interventions that you use?" He stroked his greying beard as he spoke.

"It depends on the severity. Behavioural skills for the ones who are low-functioning autistic and medication sometimes if it's like ADHD."

The professor scoffed, and I knew what was coming.

"The system overmedicates these kids, sometimes based on a misdiagnosis."

I nodded slightly and sipped my tea. I recognized this particular gripe of his from class discussions and agreed that the overdiagnosing and medicating in mental health can be dangerous. He believed in a more delicate approach to handing out diagnoses that could, depending on the community, damage a person's life prospects.

He continued. "One of my students thought I was discrediting the function of diagnoses in the field. I asked what he would think of a doctor who is known for overtreating illnesses based on erroneous diagnoses, and of course that stopped him. I then shared scholarly articles on instances where psychiatrists have zealously mislabelled ADHD."

I shook my head as I pictured the students frowning at how bluntly the professor addressed them. Blunt he was, but I had come to understand that it was a small failing when you got to know the man. He reminded me very much of the average Nigerian father—when it was time to scold you, all sentiments were to be left aside.

"Tell me again how you came to the decision to study psychology?" he said, crossing his legs in front of the table and picking up his cup of coffee.

"I'm not sure how it started exactly, but I used to read some of the things my dad would leave around the house, and this particular one that stuck with me was about how the mind can make the body do weird things. I know now that it's called psychosomatization, but I remember thinking, *Wow, that explains why I have a weak stomach when I'm scared.*"

"Weak stomach?" he asked.

"My stomach gets runny," I responded, smirking as I negotiated the right words. Apparently in America such talk is considered private; otherwise, I would have been more descriptive. There were times in childhood when I had a few accidents, and my mother put it down to my love of street food. She used to taunt me, "Samira, all this rubbish you will be buying on the road, after you will be getting typhoid and be doing fut fut in the toilet."

"So I started paying more attention to psychology movies and talk shows. I fell in love with Dr. Phil and used to dream about coming to America just to meet him." I shoved a piece of iced pound cake in my mouth and noticed the professor's eyes lingering on my plate of sweets.

"Ah, Dr. Phil." He sighed. He found it unfortunate when professionals in the field paraded themselves on TV instead of going into communities to help people.

"Anyway, I guess I loved psychology before I knew what it was about. It just makes sense of things."

He nodded. "Have you ever found any of the concepts to be contrary to your cultural beliefs?"

"Oh yes. I definitely don't agree with everything. To be honest, sometimes I wonder if some things are exaggerated or maybe the explanation is not as simple as just psychology. For example, take pica. I can understand somebody eating sand, since back home we give pregnant women potash stones to chew because it's a normal craving. But to eat batteries or metal? That seems more like a spiritual problem."

"So you think it's a bit contrived," he stated, adjusting his glasses.

"It's just that sometimes it doesn't make much sense." I made a mental note to look up the word *contrived* later and decided that was a safe response. "The thing is, sir, I know there can be a biological component to something as crazy as that, but sometimes I just feel like it's first world problems for people with stable living conditions and too much time on their hands."

If they received some good flogging like I did, they would have had focus and direction in life, I wanted to say.

"Ah," the professor said softly. "Is that how you perceived your classmates?"

Truthfully, I had found their preoccupations frivolous, like all they cared about was drinking and joining fraternities, not so much the education.

"Well, it depends. My parents would never have approved of some of the things they did, even when exams were approaching. Growing up in Nigeria, even babies in kindergarten are taught a nursery rhyme that goes like this: 'Good, better, best / I shall never rest / Till my good is better and my better best.' And so the expectation in school is that you would excel at all costs. Our teachers would compare results, pitching the As against the Bs."

"Hmm. It appears you have a certain privilege, as I find with most immigrants. You're grounded in the reality of high expectations by virtue of your immigration. It's sort of a tentpole that keeps you focused on your goals."

"I guess, but it's not easy." I scoffed. "I recall Clare saying—remember her?"

The professor nodded.

"She said she felt sorry for me because I couldn't tell when people's comments were racist."

"And how did you respond to that?"

"I mean, I'm not stupid. I have definitely experienced outright racism, but I wasn't focusing on that. My goal was to make my parents proud."

At first those conversations left me feeling like a fool and then it became irritating to have to analyse every comment about my hair or accent or whatever else. I certainly hated the ugliness of racism. As an African, it put me in a precarious position as both victim by virtue of my skin colour and perpetrator as a descendant of cowardly Blacks who sold their brothers. But all of this existed in my mind only in theory until I came to America. Then the restless dream of living happily ever after in privilege quickly became unveiled as a fantasy. I resented that and tried to distance myself from it.

"Well, the same was true in this country up until about the nineteenth century. Mental problems were treated sometimes by exorcism, so that's fair." The professor evaded the race talk, possibly sensing my unease. "And yes, pica is one of the more extreme diagnoses, but think about your community back home. Can you see any benefit to the education you now have as far as understanding some of the common issues?"

"I do when I think about it. There were many things I didn't understand before, but now I see them in a way that I wish I had back then, which brings me to something I've been wanting to ask you. What do you think of restraints for kids in a school setting?"

"Restraints?"

"Yes, like physical restraint for the kids when they become aggressive." I motioned a dip with my hands.

"Hmm. They still do that?"

"Yes, sir. It just seems counterintuitive, like we're not allowed to hold them back from running into traffic, but we're allowed to restrain them."

"Right. Do the kids get hurt?"

"Well, apparently the supine is safer."

"That's the one where they're face up, right?" I nodded in agreement, and he continued. "And the other one is prone?"

"Yeah. We don't use prone because of the risks, but even this one just kills my muscles, and I don't know if it helps."

"Sounds like a good research project for you."

"I guess." I couldn't hide my disappointment. I had already done some Google searches to see if there were other interventions that facilities used but couldn't find anything. The professor knows so much about everything that I was really looking forward to his input.

"You're there for how long again?" he asked shifting in his chair.

"Six months sir, like you suggested."

"All right. Let me know what you find." He looked at his watch and picked up his cup of coffee. "I have to head back."

I walked him to the elevator and moseyed around the ground floor before heading out. I looked forward to coming to this building just to bask in its magnificence. In the open space of the lobby, every angle showed the same structure but took you to a different arrangement that inspired imagination. Something about the daunting brilliance of the thick walls and the way it absorbed the lighting from the chandelier cast a sweet dimness over the room. I loved to study in that space. Yes, it was distracting at times when my mind wandered into the agelessness of the building, but at other times the warm ambience helped me concentrate. The gothic architecture was reminiscent of epic movies, and in time I came to realize that this was the Western world I had dreamed of one day seeing. The one where I could experience other lives in an alternate reality and the stories of the people whose collective effort created this greatness. Surely theirs was a time when honour and dignity meant everything. Yet it was not lost on me that some of the charm of that time was also clouded by atrocious acts such as the torture and molestation of mentally ill people. The chambers often made me think of secrets long buried, what with the chairs and knobs of odd figures that looked like they would someday come alive, as they did in the cartoons I grew up watching.

Dungeons and dragons.

I also looked forward to these intellectual exchanges with the professor, sipping tea and debating subjects with high-sounding words like *contrived.* This was what I went into psychology for, to be amidst such learned people, and maybe someday, like the professor, I too would be an accomplished psychologist waving my hands passionately as I lectured an eager audience on the complex mechanisms behind human behaviour. This was also what I came to this country for, to use the opportunities available for my own betterment. Not to be bogged down with racial identity. Of course, I expected to be treated unfairly, as Dahdee had been in some encounters with white people. But it took some time to understand the machine that operated around me as a Black person in the US—the system that had been designed to shape my identity and aspirations in the so-called land of the free. The professor always argued that we immigrants cannot separate ourselves from the plight of our African American colleagues. Then again, I never knew if it was more accurate to say African American or Black, so I argued that we aren't necessarily trying to do that. We were just trying to protect our own identity— that of where we come from, the names we bear that tell stories of our ancestors, the heritage that was passed on to us. This is the unique burden we carry as foreigners in the land, for whom no one will fight. Not even our brothers in skin colour. As Aunty Zubaida would always say in pidgin, "Abeg, we come from far."

I graduated from the University of Pittsburgh on a chilly spring day in April, with high hopes of becoming the next Dr. Phil. My certificate read: *Samira Adakunnaya Ofunwa, Bachelor of Science, Psychology.*

I've always gone by my first name, which was given to me by my mother. She swears it was a name she always loved, a name of such strong meaning. In truth my grandmother had insisted on that name for me, and that was that. My father, a modest Igbo man, was left with the middle name, and so he bestowed on me the honour of being his bringer of wealth. He treated me as such, always telling stories of how good things started to come to him after I was born. "Ada m" he called me, as his first daughter. I ended up being my parents' only child, apparently because my mother got a bad case of fibroid and was no longer able to conceive. Some said I had sabotaged her womb on my way out to block any future children from spoiling my affluent existence. I didn't dispute that, even though I envied my friends who had siblings.

My parents were pleased with my achievement as a university graduate but would have been more thrilled if it was a doctorate so that my mother could call me Dr. Mira before her friends.

She would have loved that. And frankly so would I. I wanted to get a doctorate in psychology, I wanted to host my own TV show and offer expert advice to troubled youth, and I even fantasized about becoming a real actress and not just a pretend one in my head. I wanted it all, and I knew I could do anything I put my mind to. I just needed inspiration.

That, and I needed to overcome a chronic case of procrastination.

Thankfully, I made it through my schooling with good grades despite my scatterbrain. Come graduation day, I was determined to mark the significance of my achievement by participating for the first time in a revered school tradition.

Riding the back of the school panther.

I walked up to it as its cold hard eyes stared down at me. The streets of Oakland had been blocked for the ceremony, and the excitement of students and parents buzzing around me faded as I came face-to-face with the black panther. I couldn't help thinking about the poor soul in history who must have, at one point, been this close to a panther's breath. A real one. Many a whispering onlooker had alluded that panthers once roamed free in this city way back in time. Now even as the school mascot, it still commanded awe and respect.

Dressed in blood orange pants and a mustard blouse, I got behind the queue with other aspiring climbers, dusting up my graduation gown and preparing for my picture moment on the beast. In my four years of schooling, I had watched students of all calibres climb that slick back stealthily like it was nothing. So I was ready for my turn. How hard could it be?

"Make sure you wave your cap too!" Muhmee shouted to me. I was determined to do that and even throw it in celebratory eagerness. When it came time, I climbed the statue ledge with much effort, as I realized that it was a little higher than I had thought and than my short legs were ready for. With help from Muhmee, I managed to hoist myself onto the panther's back by holding on to the steel belly, cold from the lingering frost of winter. As I shifted to balance my stiletto heels for a pose, my thin graduation gown slipped on the steel, and I just about had the fall of my life. My ankle gave in, and the skinny heel of my shoe broke, thankfully making for a somewhat better footing. Just like that my picture moment was ruined. All I could manage was an awkward smile as people prompted me to lift that broken shoe in the air like a champ. I should have known the panther did not approve of that graduation ritual; it would not have surprised me at all if it had roused to life and tossed me to the ground, shattering my brain and dignity.

And so a broken heel was the culmination of my undergraduate life, a failure that almost embodied my struggles as an immigrant. It was ironic that the one person to fail what seemed like a causal attempt for others would be me, the supposed African princess who grew up frolicking with lions in my backyard. Legend had it that mine was a typical African childhood that saw me in the midst of lion fraternity. That was until one day when a rogue member of the lion clan attacked my cousin and then her prince charming appeared to overcome it with a death dealing clay stone in hand, thus breaking apart the brotherhood. I plagiarized that story from the one person whose quick wit had no patience for stupid questions: Aunty Zubaida.

Left with the question of what to do with a psych degree, I consulted my mentor, Professor Bodorf, who recommended that I go back to the children's centre I interned at in my third year to gain some clarity.

"I just don't see how I can make money with it unless I become a specialty therapist and partner with insurance companies or become a professor like you," I would complain, sitting across from him at the school cafeteria.

"You go into the field with the heart and for the heart," the professor would respond humbly, as if his bank account would reflect that.

Such wise words. I had a heart; it just seemed to be all over the place. I felt sorry for the kids I worked with at the centre and was happy to contribute in any way to their well-being. I just hoped it would look good enough on my résumé for future pursuits.

So I took the professor's advice and started volunteering at the Kerr Child Development Centre, hoping to find inspiration that would open my mind to the exact career opportunity to quench my thirst for greatness. The centre ran a residential program for children primarily with an autism diagnosis and other behavioural issues. When families struggled to cope with their child whose uniqueness brought them too much conflict and discomfort, that's where they turned to for help. The children received educational support on an adjusted curriculum and social skills training with the goal of rehabilitating them to be reintroduced to their community. I volunteered at the residential building but didn't have proper clearance for the school.

That was how I came to be lying on the grass crushing a young boy's legs under my weight.

"Okay, it's not bad," my parents said when I informed them, secretly wondering when I would start working and be financially independent.

That was the American way, and even though they, and myself, would say that it was more Nigerian to let me stay at home until I got married, my parents knew that the progressive thing would be to encourage me to get a part-time job and move out of their house. Aunty Zubaida, on the other hand, thought I was being spoiled and advised that if I wanted to get a master's degree, I do so quickly so as not to push back my deadline to get married.

I appreciated the fact that my parents didn't hassle me about not having a job, but I knew they wanted nothing more than for me to be something great. It would be a fair compensation for their slaving away at work and giving up major comforts so that I could finish four years of schooling and not be shackled with student loans.

But there were the occasional digs, especially from Muhmee when she just returned from working the night shift, tired and grouchy.

"My friend, you need to get a job so that you will appreciate all my suffering in this America," she would start.

"Ahnahn, Muhmee. Don't worry. I'm working on something big that will give you and Dahdee an early retirement," I would tease.

"It should better happen quickly because I'm tired of working when my mates are flexing in Nigeria!" Muhmee would retort.

"Muhmee, at least thank God you had only me. What if you still had three more children to train?"

"Ehn, more people to take care of me, nau, more money when I retire. If you had become a doctor or something, that one would have been my compensation."

I really should have become a doctor or an engineer if there would be any chance at reimbursing my parents. I owed them that much for their heavy investment in my education. Especially since I was their only child, their only hope. But those careers didn't interest me. I lived and breathed all things psychology.

When I was a junior in secondary school in Nigeria, insignificant and listless, I never would have dreamed that I would one day be taught in a prestigious institution such as the University of Pittsburgh.

That too at the glorious cathedral of learning.

Every time I walked through the dome to enter the building, I instantly felt like I was stepping onto a movie set. There were often other people who were equally enthralled and soaking up the wonder as they made their way to different orders of business. I got to rub shoulders with people of varied nationalities, and some of them, with camera in hand, spoke in unfamiliar languages that indicated they were tourists. Those were my people, the ones who got it. I liked them more than the typical crowd during the school semester made up of skimpily dressed students whose heads would be buried in their phones while architectural glory wasted away around them. In my school days when I wasn't studying, I would tuck myself into a spot in one of the miniature chambers and dream of what could have been of the place in the past. I loved how the little corners with random stairs were so cosy and inviting of mischief. Walking through the common area, it was paradoxical to me that the dimly lit lobby often had students huddled close to study, and yet with the books in front of them, there was always a sense of lascivious intent diffusing through the air.

The concepts I learned in my classes taught me things that opened my eyes, things that only made sense in the context of psychology. For instance, it helped me realize that perhaps there was an undiagnosed autistic in my own family.

It was my aunt, Dahdee's older sister. I had a faint memory of this aunt, whom I had seen in the village only through the window of the room where she was locked up. The story I heard then was of how Aunty was a madwoman who needed to be contained to avoid any harm to herself or others.

But what exactly is the nature of the madness? I often wondered as I became an adult.

Dahdee explained at different times that Aunty was born with limited speaking ability as well as some "strange behaviours" that got worse as she got older. She never married or had children and was attached to her mother's hip her whole life. At some point it seemed like Aunty would get better but then out of nowhere she had a severe bout of illness. One day after that, she lunged at her mother as she was eating a plate of hot rice, leaving her with a nasty burn. That was how she came to be locked up, and by the time I would see her as a child, she was nothing more than a caged problem reduced to animalistic growls and isolation in a dark, smelly existence.

I had so many questions about my aunt but did not have the courage to ask my parents. Occasionally I would get a flashback of her face staring longingly at me through the louvres and then the corner of her mouth would twitch as her weather-worn features relaxed.

"Samira, come down from there. You will fall!" she would warn when I climbed everything in sight.

Her voice still resounded in my head, soft and slow but certain. Sometimes those memories seemed made up, like I was drawing a picture of what never existed. My parents verified that I had been in proximity with this aunt, but they could not confirm the exact encounters. I thought about the person my aunt would have been. Deep down, what was she like? What did she fantasize about? What annoyed her or made her happy? What did she think of her family? Of me as a kid? Dahdee had told me that every time he called back home to the village, they told him that Aunty asked for all the family by name, including me. The thought of that, how isolated and forgotten this aunt had become while still alive, was too much for me to process, so I didn't think about it for a long time.

Until the day that Dahdee came home and broke the news that his sister had died, his face a shadow of emotions that I could not read. It occurred to me then what a waste it was not to have known that aunt personally. How could I truly mourn the loss of a person who was certainly precious but who was a stranger to me? I processed these thoughts with Professor Bodorf, at the beginning of my third year, pointing out that the horror of my aunt being locked up is the norm in Nigeria for people with such strange conditions.

What if it was autism? I came to wonder when I learned about the diagnosis in class. The story of my aunt's presentation made it seem likely—the rocking back and forth, hands shaking, and muttering in repetitive sounds. Perhaps there was something else too, maybe a learning disability or some underlying mental problem. When I broached the subject with Dahdee, he was surprisingly open to discussion about it but hesitant to accept that it may have been that simple.

"Ah well, you know America is very good at analysing such things, better than we are," he said dismissively.

It was never known if my aunt had autism when she died. But I became interested in autism in adults and wrote my undergrad thesis on the subject. Professor Bodorf had approved the paper and encouraged me to pursue further education in the field of autism. I appreciated the insight into my aunt's condition, but I wasn't convinced that it was quite the direction I wanted to go in.

So there I was, unmarried at twenty-four, still living with my parents, jobless, and with no idea what to do with my life.

Chapter 2

CHOP BELLEFUL

idowa hated the days I would meet with the professor. He swore it was only because he couldn't reach me, but I knew he was jealous. Not for good reason because he had learned to trust me after going steady for the six years I lived in the US.

Well, for most of the six years.

During my undergrad studies, I looked forward to getting his messages throughout the day and giving him a play-by-play of what I was doing.

I had on my favourite outfit—a snug Arsenal jersey on top of a short pleated skirt paired with white sneakers. I always felt like a total babe dressed like that. I only wished I had more chest to fill it out.

If I wore this outfit on the streets of Lagos, I would have gotten a lot of shout-outs, horns tooting for me, and people hollering the signature Arsenal fan call—*Gunners for life!*

I missed that about Nigeria. I missed the culture of football watching and fan community. As an Arsenal fan, I would have known just where to go for some camaraderie.

My phone would buzz in my pocket as I settled into my classes, and I knew who it was before I even looked at it.

Midowa.

The first time I realized that the cathedral had dead zones and would seize his messages was after I gave him hell for not responding right away.

How far babe! I read off BBM messenger.

I sent him a frowny face in response and slipped the phone back in my pocket as the professor was about to begin. I itched for the hour and a half before break to look at my phone, but I was not going to be that girl.

Ahnahn, why the face nau? Midowa had written.

Didn't hear from you all day and "how far babe" is all you can say? My fingers were typing quicker than my brain could come up with a retort.

Nooo baby I sent you messages since, I said maybe you're busy.

I looked back through my phone, and sure enough there were unread messages from the morning when I accused him of ignoring me.

I told you I was at that meeting all day nau.

I knew you'd be sleeping. Meanwhile there was no light and my battery died.

Sorry nau. How are you?

Answer me nauuuu.

The string of messages poured in, and even though I felt bad for being a brat, I decided with deviousness in my heart that I quite enjoyed his restless pining. And so it became a game that I would send him messages when I walked into the building and make him wait for a response. In truth I was waiting too, as every now and then, a flash of phone signal would creep into a corner of the building, and I would catch it if I was positioned just right.

The perils of long-distance relationships.

After I graduated, he assumed that I would no longer be confined to the school building and would get frustrated when he still couldn't reach me. But I was continuing to meet with the professor after graduation and would try to call him as soon as I got out.

I took out my phone and called him.

"My baby." He sounded winded, like he had picked up the phone a little too hurriedly.

"Go, jor," I replied, my voice heavy with playful sulking.

"Oya, sorry nau, my love, don't vex for me ejoo." He had learned to just apologize even if he didn't know what for. I quite enjoyed the pain in his voice.

"Hmm, okay oooo." I wasn't going to make it easy for him. It turned out that after so long of doing the same dance, I had to stir the pot to keep things interesting.

"It's good to hear your voice."

"What, my siiiilvery voice?" I mocked.

"Yes, baby, your silvery voice." He chuckled. He first told me that early in our long-distance relationship, and it sounded like it was straight out of a novel. He added that my voice was like crisp, clean water being poured into an aluminium basin. The sheer romance.

"How are you, love? How was the meeting?" I asked.

He hissed. "It was okay jare. Normal yarns."

"So what did your uncle say?"

"He said I should call him by the end of the week."

"Pele, my love, I hope it works out."

"Me too. I'm tired of this runs." I pictured him lying in bed in their family-owned bungalow, shirtless in the sweltering heat of Lagos after a day half-spent at work and half-wasted in traffic.

"My dear, the patient dog eats the fattest bone, so just hold on." His uncle was going to get him some kind of promotion. Thank God for the man even being in that firm; he would have otherwise been stuck in the rut of unemployed youth in Lagos.

"How was your time with the professor?"

"Good. We had a nice chat about the cross section between public and mental health."

"You sha like all this educative talk. Anyway, that's one good thing about America, una dey chop belleful. Nobody has time in Nigeria; too much suffering."

By chop belleful he was referring to the general privilege that Nigerians perceive of the Western world. When people have basic needs met, they tend to aspire to great and abstract ventures. In Nigeria the fight was still at the bottom for the basics, so such conversationing seemed frivolous.

While I would light a candle in my room to create a scented cosy ambience, Midowa would be lighting a candle to see his papers while he worked on his architectural project. Such were the differences in our realities and would be reflected in the way we approached conversations.

"Well, that's Maslow's theory," I responded, having taught him the concept of Maslow's hierarchy from the time I first learned it in Psychology 101. It was interesting and explained a lot to me as far as the contrast between life in Nigeria and the US.

"The basic human needs like food and water are at the base of the pyramid and must be satisfied first before a person becomes preoccupied with other concerns. So the lower-level needs must be met before people become more interested in the higher levels. As for the almighty peak of self-actualization, it's hard to imagine in Nigeria when steady power and water supply are still a luxury." Midowa would listen to me recite my textbook and chime in with a question.

"So is that like the adage that a person whose house is on fire doesn't chase rats?"

"Yup. I think that explains it. Safety first and then you can worry about aesthetics."

"Mira, Mira, I hope that your professor is not tripping for this your brain o," he teased.

"Abeg o, that man is a daddy. He's not thinking about me."

"What of my husband, Tega?" I asked.

"Ah, he's okay now, thank God." Midowa's younger brother and only sibling was a chubby, sweet little kid who had just suffered a case of typhoid and malaria. I missed patting his cheeks and watching his defiant mouth protrude in annoyance.

"Are you not my husband again?" I would tease and pout my lips like I was going to kiss his cheeks. I always wondered what it would be like to have siblings, a brother especially. Sure, Aunty Zubaida was as much a sibling to me as any, but the fact that I called her aunty created some undeniable boundaries.

"Hehn, don't kiss me oo!" young Tega would warn, spit flying into the air because of his lisp. The freedom to carry on such characteristic banter in Nigeria was one of the things I missed when I traded home for life in the US of A.

"What of Aunty Zubaida?" Midowa asked.

"She's fine oo, no crisis since." Aunty Zubaida had sickle cell anaemia, and it is the Nigerian language of love to ask about family members regarding their respective illnesses.

"Really, thank God o!" He sucked his teeth, and I pictured him shaking his head in pity. "At least she is in America now. I'm sure they have a better way of managing it over there."

"Ehn, well, true sha. Maybe your brother needs to come here too so that he will stop falling sick."

Even as I said that, I knew I was talking rubbish. But that's what you say when you speak to people back home with any ailments—you assure them that if they could just find their way to America, their problem would be solved. I hated that mindset, and yet here I was endorsing it.

"Na so, that's how my uncle was gisting us that he made the mistake of telling his doctor he had malaria from his last visit to Naija. Oh boy, he said he ended up with a bill of over five thousand dollars for whatever treatment they gave him. That is on top of quarantining him like somebody who had leprosy." Midowa scoffed. "Anyway, they have their own specialty over there; we too have our own."

I knew he was right but took issue with the way he always said *over there*, like it's a different world isolated from reality. Reality that I was now so privileged to be removed from.

"Yeah, tor I'm getting on the bus now. Just wanted to say hi," I said to dismiss him.

"You did well, babe. Just buzz me when you're home." By the time I got home, he would likely be fast asleep. Such was the dance of a six-hour time difference long-distance relationship.

"I will. Bye, hon." I hung up and walked out of the building to catch the bus. I picked up my steps as other students dragged their feet along the crossing lines. They all looked so entitled, like they could crawl through the crossing and there would be nothing said by impatient motorists. Now graduated, I wondered if I had been just as listless in crossing the street. How did they all manage to look so chill when they had classes to get to? I couldn't picture myself being that way, but something told me I had fit in with the floating crowd.

I stepped forward as the bus groaned to a stop in front of me. With one last look at the building behind, I took a mental photo of the beautiful back drop as evening encroached on the height of the impressive skyscraper. I caught my reflection in the bus window and adjusted my braids, full with baby hairs almost touching my eyebrows. I studied the face in the reflection, the face that Midowa called his jewel, with my wide forehead and soft brown eyes that sat above a delicately planted nose. Midowa would gently cup his hands under my pointed chin and examine my face from all angles. Under his gaze I used to feel like a rare diamond. As a child, people would pull at my apple cheeks and call me a fine girl. Living in America, I never heard that expression anymore, and so I concluded that perhaps I wasn't all that.

Midowa was a typical Lagos boy from a middle-class family, fresh by opinion but still aware that he needed to step up his game to fit into some circles. His parents had lived in Lagos all their lives and raised their kids there. He learned from the incredible diversity of the city to transition well from one setting to the next. He could put on his urban Lagos accent for work and other corporate affairs and then switch to a husky street boy pidgin with his guys. I always marvelled at the way he spoke Yoruba like it was his native tongue while only managing a few loose expressions in his father's Urhobo and his mother's Itsekiri. My friends called him handsome, with his angular cheekbones and hooded eyes framed by prescription glasses. He worked in an architectural firm as a junior employee with his uncle. He looked the part of a professional nerd, but to me he was the boy who was obsessed with the Goo Goo Dolls and burned a mixed-rock CD for his girlfriend as a parting gift.

The day before we left for the US, I went to see him at his house, and his parents teased that they would make sure he came to the States to join me. We stayed in his room to chat while his brother, Tega, played football outside.

"Please tell him to give it to me nau, ahnahn. What is a boy doing with colourful neck beads sef?" I lamented to Midowa, looking out the window of his room at his brother playing with his friends.

"See this, babe o. The boy made the beads as a class project, and you expect him to just give it to you?" Midowa replied with a smile, knowing that his argument was moot and that I would eventually get those beads. He couldn't resist me and would part with anything at my command. He said that I was a magnet and in due time all good things propel towards me. Midowa swore his brother liked me, but he was always hiding when I came around.

"Tell him I will marry him if he gives it to me." I grinned, raising my eyebrows simultaneously.

He started laughing. That always made him smile.

"You know how stubborn that boy is. He would love to just collect iyawo egbon e, his brother's wife." He eyed me from the computer chair where he was sitting.

"Listen, tell him there is nothing on this finger." I raised my ring finger to his face. "That necklace will make me so happy." I strolled dramatically towards him, sitting on his lap and throwing my arms around his neck.

"So if he lets me have it, then egbon to dull ni. He will pay the bride price." Midowa was rubbing off on me with his Yoruba.

"Pay the bride price bawo? He's seven. He should go and sit down. This one na my own." He reached his nose to touch mine and pulled back to look at my face. I was no longer smiling.

I stood up and walked back to the window.

He followed me. "I know what you're thinking," he said softly behind me, his fingers scratching my arms lightly. The room was throbbing with stifling heat. I wanted him close. I just didn't like the tingle of his sweaty palm on my bare skin.

I turned around to face him.

"I don't know when or if I'm coming back. What's going to happen to us?" I avoided his eyes. Glancing up, I saw that they burned behind his glasses, heavy with emotion.

Midowa sighed. "Baby, I don't know honestly. I think about that every second. But you know what, I don't want to spoil your joy for now. This is good—you are going to America! Let's see what God is planning for us. If anything happens, at least I know that you have been my happiness for two years, and that's enough for me."

"Not me." I felt weak turning around to the window and staring off into the distance.

That was the last time I saw Midowa in person, and it seemed like a perfectly romantic note to end on. Somehow, we were still talking about having a future together after eight years of knowing eachother. Midowa would always mention all the questions his friends asked while I reminded him that a young man in his prime had no business waiting on a girl who is abroad.

"So what are you people planning to do? Will you go and meet her abroad? Would she be willing to move back home? Is this relationship even real?" they would ask.

We asked ourselves those very same questions, so I didn't blame them.

To be fair we had done quite well with the torture of long-distance communication. By the fifth year, it had started wearing on the light-heartedness we enjoyed before I left home, but we were both determined to make it work. When we were in secondary school, we had to use NITEL landlines to call each other and would some-times leave messages with family members. We gradually moved from talking over landlines to Yahoo and MSN messenger, and by the time we graduated, I had upgraded to a cell phone. Midowa would borrow his dad's cell phone to text me or, on occasion, to call. Thankfully, by 2001, GSM broke into Nigeria, so most individuals could own cell phones for their personal use.

Now with the BlackBerry craze, it was easy to call or text anyone abroad and even video chat. It was good enough, considering that we had no communication for five months at some point when I came to the States. I was too distracted to really feel the gap, but Midowa said it was very hard for him. Thanks to the advances in technology, all he had to do was make sure his phone was fully charged with power and credit, and he was good.

Some people would say I was just stringing him along, but I didn't want to make a mistake. I needed to be sure of what I was doing. Muhmee knew he and I had a thing, but she never asked about it once I left Nigeria.

—~—~—

"Muhmee, good evening, ma!" I got home from grocery shopping and shut the front door cheerfully only to see my mother pacing the kitchen floor, shouting at someone on the phone. I could hear Dahdee shuffling his feet in the room upstairs.

"Answer me, Zubaida. Has he paid your bride price? *Mutuniyar banza*. Walahi if you know what is good for you, ehn, you will carry yourself back to your house and respect yourself before you disgrace me. Gaskiya you will see yourself with this nonsense you call life. Just quote me walahi, quote me!" Her anger punctuated by the melody of a prominent Fulani lilt was on full display.

When I came to the US, I realized how regretful it was that I never learned to speak either of my parents' languages beyond some loose expressions. Dahdee left us in Nigeria just when I was old enough to start making an effort. I wasn't particularly close to his side of the family and rarely got to travel to the village. Life cheated me out of knowing his parents who died in a car accident when I was about two years old. As for Muhmee, her roots were so twisted, I wasn't even sure what tribal group to identify with. While her mother's native tongue was Igala, she grew up speaking Hausa, which her mother had adopted. Growing up in Lagos, I was surrounded by people who spoke different languages, and so the only Hausa I ever learned was my mother's fiery expressions of frustration or colourful descriptions of my foolishness.

Muhmee pushed her thumb so hard to end the call that I felt sure a finger bone had snapped. Aunty Zubaida was a force to be reckoned with, and sometimes that force put her big sister's ire in overdrive. I was already used to conversations like this one involving her younger sister, Zubaida. Aunty Zubaida, the one I had diagnosed with oppositional defiant disorder, was one of my favourite characters in the world. She always got up to something that would make her sister upset, yet somehow she managed to remain the apple of her eye. I knew my mother loved me, but I also knew that Aunty Zubaida shared equal bragging rights in the family. She held a solid spot in her big sister's heart.

"Ehen, my dear. How are you?" Muhmee's voice dropped a few decibels. That was the way a Nigerian woman would respond to her child's greeting after an altercation with another person. The softer tone was an indication that you were in a favourable position with her and not be getting yelled at. Until of course, you happen to slip up and become the next target.

"I'm fine muhmee." I put away the grocery bags while she muttered words like *nonsense disgrace* and clattered pots and pans with a force that testified to her great annoyance. I debated if I should ask what my dear aunty Zubaida had done but decided I would wait until she told me. It would have been rude to ask and would indicate that I did not have enough respect to know that whatever my aunty had done was grown-up talk between my parents, unless I was invited.

I did get invited.

Muhmee laughed in mockery and clapped her hands together as if dusting off some powder. "There is nothing I will not see!" The narrative was coming.

"Can you imagine, Zubaida has moved in with the man who has been promising to marry her since God knows when? Ehn, this same man who has not even finished divorcing his wife."

I was putting away the milk and other items, planning in my head how best to respond to this information like I didn't already know it. I debated whether to say *Ah!* in dramatic exclamation or to just chime in a *hmm* in acknowledgment that this act on my aunty's part was especially incredulous. For a sickler, Aunty Zubaida was unbelievably daring, but then again her health condition often left her teetering between life and death.

Legend had it that Muhmee was born in Kano, where Grandma Ufi was trying to make a life for herself having escaped nothingness. Grandma had lived there for two years. She was an attractive, vibrant nineteen-year-old Igala woman trying to hustle and find a man to make a home with. She fit nicely with the Hausa people whose language and culture she had always loved. People had told her growing up that she looked like a northerner, so learning the Hausa language was all she needed to blend in. She had met a nicelooking Alhaji who promised to make her a second wife. According to Muhmee, Grandma Ufi had a whirlwind romance with this Alhaji and did everything to get him to commit to marrying her. Everything short of taking up his Muslim faith, that is. She thought she had convinced him that religion didn't matter and that love would triumph, until the day he whisked her away to a lonely park and told her that he had too much to lose by marrying her. He had broken up with her that night and, in a strange twist, threatened that if she did not distance herself from him, there would be consequences. Grandma Ufi had revealed to him that she was pregnant, and she was going to keep the baby; she begged him not to abandon her and the child. He had called her a loose woman and accused her of carrying someone else's child. Zooming off in his nice Mercedes, he left her sobbing in the cloud of brown dirt from the road. When Muhmee was born, Grandma Ufi had taken the baby to the Alhaji's house to show him that the child looked just like him. She never even made it into the compound, as the Alhaji instructed the guard not to open the gate.

And so Grandma Ufi took her child back to the communal accommodation where other women were waiting to commiserate with her and help her raise the baby. They had offered her diabolical ways to trap the Alhaji and have him granting her every wish. Grandma Ufi had apparently refused this offer and mourned her loss. She never got over the Alhaji, and apparently he never got over her either. They would go on to meet at different times, with Grandma Ufi still vying for position as his wife and the Alhaji still wanting to have his cake and eat it too.

Fast-forward twenty years later. Grandma Ufi was forty-two years old and running a successful fabrics trade she got pregnant for a second time. It was the same Alhaji, who somehow had lured her again with the promise of marriage. When Muhmee told the story, she said that at this point, Grandma Ufi must have known that she would never be his wife but was somehow so spellbound by him that she kept going back to be disgraced. Did the community never find out about this? What about his other wives? What about her parents in Kogi state? I thought those questions but never dared to ask. I had only heard this story told to other adults; it was never directed to me. I was, after all, just a child.

By then Muhmee was staying with her aunty in Lagos, something that she had always dreamed of, perhaps in imitation of her mother, who likewise left home to seek adventures. Grandma Ufi, ashamed of being pregnant at her age and under such circumstances, decided to go to Lagos for the duration of the pregnancy. She stayed with her sister, whose life was a stark contrast to hers, living with her husband and young children in a standard nuclear family. Muhmee had helped her mother throughout the pregnancy, taking care of her, as the woman was quite spoiled. She even helped her to the point of delivery and beyond, taking care of the baby for whom she felt both pity and disappointment. This poor baby was born in circumstances even worse than hers. Muhmee had never known her father, except for the stories in the streets, and had made her peace with her life. And now her mother had made a more terrible mistake by giving birth to this child in her old age. Even worse, the child turned out to be a sickler because Grandma, in her blind obsession, missed the fact that the Alhaji, just like her, was carrying the sickle cell gene. Grandma Ufi had named the baby Zubaida, after one of the daughters of the Alhaji. Muhmee hated the idea but decided to give up the fight. She resented her mother for bringing this child into what would be a pathetic existence but somehow found it in her heart to forgive her carelessness.

Grandma Ufi had taken baby Zubaida back to Kano with a very intriguing story that it was in fact her daughter's illegitimate baby whom she was going to raise as her own. Aunty Zubaida knew that Grandma Ufi was her mother but was not allowed to tell anyone that. So when her sister came to visit, she had to pretend that was her mother. Muhmee did not approve of the charade but never stayed with her mother long enough to challenge it. Indeed, she cared for Aunty Zubaida like a daughter and hoped that life would compensate her for an unfortunate beginning.

I thought that Aunty Zubaida had been sent to live with her sister due to better medical care for managing her sickle cell, but the whispers I heard between my parents suggested that there had been some incident where Aunty Zubaida was caught in a compromising situation with a boy in an uncompleted building. Grandma Ufi had been concerned about what would become of the girl and shipped her off to live with her sister. By the time Aunty Zubaida came to stay with us, I had visited Grandma Ufi only three times. As I got older, it became apparent to me that Grandma Ufi had always wanted someone else to raise Zubaida.

After dinner, Muhmee was still talking Dahdee to death about Zubaida this and Zubaida that while I searched Google for articles on physical restraints in mental health, trying not to laugh. I looked up occasionally to shake my head as Muhmee's face contorted in horror, coaxing Dahdee to mirror her anger. How unfortunate it was that Aunty Zubaida's lifestyle caused her sister so much grief, and yet she continued to do these things. There was never any respite between her having a health crisis and being a crisis herself.

Dahdee's phone rang. It was someone at work, and it sounded like it would take longer than a few minutes because he shifted from his arched position facing Muhmee and placed his elbows on his knees while he spoke. Muhmee called me to help her store the leftover dinner in the fridge. I immediately jumped up to join her in the kitchen, knowing I was on slippery ground with her. After an incident like this, there was always the potential that I would get on her nerves without trying. When Aunty Zubaida lived with us, it would have been my entertainment to see Muhmee's anger fully charged towards her, always the culprit. Now being the only child in the house meant that I had to pacify her to the highest degree.

I started to tell her something funny, but just as I put my phone on the kitchen countertop, it buzzed in her line of sight.

I froze as her eyes darted towards the phone that was inches away from her.

"Baby? Who is calling you baby?" She glared at me as I snatched the phone and looked to see that it was a BBM message from Midowa.

Jeez, why is he still up? Of all the luck that he would text me in that moment with Muhmee standing right there.

"No o, Muhmee, it's Midowa, my friend in Nigeria. You know him." My voice was a few pitches too high.

"And he is texting you by this time?" She scoffed. "You girls should just be misbehaving. So you're still talking to that boy?" She clapped her hands and continued. "I hope you are not thinking of going back to Nigeria to meet him, ehn. Better focus on your future o, hehn. Look at your aunty Zubaida. Don't be like her oo because I will not forgive you. Wani shiririta ne wanan!" She clattered pots and pans in the sink and mumbled under her breath as she left the kitchen.

I hurried through my chores and disappeared into my room, listening for when Muhmee would tell on me. After being so discreet about my relationship with Midowa, it finally came to light at the worst possible time. My parents had strict values, and it was really bold of Aunty Zubaida to shun them the way she did. I needed them to know that I was not her. I would never be.

Chapter 3

NIGERIAN DREAM

When we first arrived in the US, five years after Dahdee, I initially felt like I was living my wildest dream and never wanted to wake up. It was the year 2005. I was eighteen years old, and it was six months after my secondary school graduation.

Dahdee had won the visa lottery and was hoping to work as a radio presenter in America. His previous job was at a radio station as the morning show guy. I bragged about it to my friends constantly.. Dahdee told us that his boss made a recommendation for him to work in Oklahoma at a radio station. His plan was to start the process for us to come over after he got situated with the job.

The story went that on his arrival in the US, he stayed with a Nigerian family who were good friends with his former boss. He was not happy with the lack of Nigerian or African presence in the state. Worse yet, he had found out that the radio program offer was not what it appeared to be. He had followed up with his boss's contact at the station, but the offer ended up being a competition that he was eventually shut out of. He was told that his accent was too thick, how could Americans understand it? This baffled him greatly, as he was sure that none of those people in competition with him were pronouncing words correctly, in the Queen's English way. He would later come to understand the politics of race in America and how it affected his work options.

Dahdee was not an impressive-looking man. He was five ten and light skinned. The timbre of his voice was what made him stand out, and he wanted nothing more than to use it in some capacity. He decided to move to another state to pursue other opportunities. He relocated to Texas, where there was a bigger Nigerian community, and he found that although the connection exposed him to some resources like the African food market, it also exposed him to some dangerous company with sleazy job offers. A Good Samaritan then offered to get him into the nursing field because that is really the only way for a Nigerian to make it in America. He declined, sticking to his guns. It became a long, drawn-out battle as he moved from state to state, auditioning at different radio stations, even trying out an apprenticeship. He soon learned that a degree from an American university in media/broadcasting would be required in addition to his Nigeria-obtained mass communication degree to pursue a radio career. After a long struggle, he decided that as strong as his passion was, it made more sense to follow the advice of others and do something that would pay him well.

Nursing.

He gave it his best shot, but after two semesters he confirmed that he indeed had a strong aversion to the medical sciences. He quit nursing school and switched to a master's in business administration, working side jobs and saving like his life depended on it. All the while he heavily resented that no one in his new home was all that impressed with his golden voice.

Meanwhile, we waited for him back home, believing that he had applied for us to join him and that it was just taking forever. In reality it wasn't until his third year in the US, after he finished graduate school and started working, that he put in the family-based green card application. Muhmee was disappointed to find this out but understood that he did not want us to come to America to suffer. Dahdee had thought that when he applied, it would be approved within a year. The process turned out to be more complex after 9/11, and it seemed like the finish line had been moved even further. Year after year, I pestered my mother, asking if we were finally making any headway. I wondered why Dahdee could not come home to visit in the meantime and asked repeatedly over pouty phone calls. He would complain about how fed up he was that the immigration process was keeping him stuck in America and then assure me that he was going to come soon. My secondary school graduation was about a year away, and I swore I would not forgive him if he dared miss it. He did miss it. In fact, our reunion at Washington's Dulles International Airport was the first time I would see my father since he came to the US.

I was disappointed to find that Dahdee was working as a real estate agent in America. What happened to the cool media dreams that we had nursed together? How easily he became an immigrant nobody when a whole fan base in Nigeria remembered his name. As the daughter of Omeraa Ofunwa, I had a protected identity, a standard to aspire to and a name to uphold. I had daydreamed many times that the voice I heard over the radio in America would one day be my father's, as it had been on our early-morning commute in Nigeria. No one had a better voice than my father's baritone, a voice that commanded respect in a refined, authoritative way. Dahdee's voice in Nigeria seemed to carry through the air, affecting whatever space he was in. In America, his orotund voice seemed almost flat, as inconsequential as a deflated balloon. Still, Dahdee maintained his casual coolness as he started to build his business, polishing that phonetic sound he had acquired from imitating television and movie characters. I missed the days when I was a small child and he taught me to transcribe words as they appear in the dictionary and pronounce them correctly. Every time I got perfect scores in

English class, I couldn't wait to tell Dahdee. Although he approved of this efficiency, he encouraged me to think deeply about my career choices. He did not heavily suggest I follow any particular career path but wanted me to excel at something sensible.

I never made peace with the way things turned out for my father. It pained me that in America when I introduce myself, my surname, a significant part of my identity, means nothing to anyone. All they see is the colour of my skin, an identity that they can summarize in one word: oppressed.

"Hey, girl!" my friend Nayana chirped as she approached me at the park entrance. It was a crisp spring evening, and the air carried a slight heaviness of summer. We had both agreed we were in need of a lazy workout regimen and decided to meet up after work once a week for walks. Nayana clicked the key fob of her Kia Sorento to make sure it was locked.

"Seriously, eyelashes?" I asked, noticing that she had decorated her headlights with long black strips that almost looked like they could blink.

"So people know it's a girl car," she twittered.

I still took the bus everywhere and swore that I don't drive because parking was too much of a hassle. Nayana tried a couple of times to get me to drive for practice, but I was too nervous about crashing her precious baby and would decline.

"How far?" she teased as we walked into the park, hearing the birds singing and the children laughing. There were many others like us milling about and soaking up the sweetness in the cool air that, in a matter of weeks, would turn into a dense thickness.

"Oooh, look at you, hmm I dey oo," I responded, proud that she had learned the pleasantries common on the streets of Nigeria.

I met Nayana at the Black students' party in second year, and we became fast friends. Not really—I practically helicoptered over her that evening, feeling a sense of kinship between us. For all intents and purposes, it was inevitable that we would become friends, seeing as she was easy to persuade. I had always wanted another Nigerian friend, and Nayana came along, never mind that she didn't really identify as Nigerian.

We both graduated from the University of Pitt, me with a BA in psychology and Nayana with a BA in photography. While I was still doing volunteer work two months after graduation, Nayana had found actual work at a small agency photographing baby products. We had our Nigerian roots in common, but her strong American ways contrasted my Nigerian reality. Nayana was born and bred in Baltimore, (by this point she had learned the Nigerian "bread and buttered" reference thanks to me) but her family moved to Pittsburgh when her dad got a job offer in postal services. Unlike me, who had known only Pittsburgh in my six years of being in the States, Nayana had moved around and was unenthused about the quiet city that had nothing to offer in comparison to Baltimore, which she called home. She did not know, nor did she care much for, anything that had to do with Nigeria.

I didn't totally blame Nayana for her lack of culturedness. Her mother had apparently named her after a favourite Indian friend, like she could not find any pretty names from Edo state to give her daughter. And so without a Nigerian name to really ground her, Nayana didn't care much about her Nigerian heritage. It was all the same to her as any other third world country. Her parents had tried to keep some tradition in their home, so she knew about the music as well as those very Nigerian expressions that our parents used. At least she had a traditional-sounding surname: Osabuohien. It served her so right, for every time she cringed at that last name, she was reminded that it was the blood that flowed in her veins.

We stopped for some ice cream on the way back to my house for our monthly weekend sleepover. The tradition went like this: We would help Muhmee with dinner and eat with my parents before retiring to my room for some reflective musings in a tranquil ambience. Except that Nayana was not really into that order of events, so some of those nights ended with her listening to her iPod, eyes glued to her phone, while I resentfully watched a Nigerian movie on my laptop.

I turned on my starlight night lamp, and with the blue and green stars swirling around us, Nayana updated me on the latest issues with her boyfriend. I scoffed internally at her foolishness but tried to be understanding.

"Listen, Naya, you can't expect him to act any differently when he has shown you from the beginning that he doesn't have sense." I launched into my usual rant to which Nayana only half listened. She was lying on my bed while I was on the floor, both of us gazing at the migrating stars dancing around the ceiling in the dark room.

"Tuh, you wouldn't understand," she said, rolling her eyes.

"Girl, please don't make excuses. That boy just sounds like bad news."

"Yeah, I don't know if I should be taking relationship advice from someone who has had only an imaginary one."

I inhaled sharply, deciding whether to take the bait. I was a few months older than Nayana, and even though she towered over me, I appointed myself prefect to catch her up on the home training she was sorely lacking.

I sighed. "What do you want out of life, Nayana?"

Silence. I looked towards the bed to see if she was on her phone. I couldn't tell but knew that it would only be a matter of time before she zoned out on me. The blue-green lighting cast a dreamy hue around the room, and as much as Nayana pretended otherwise, I knew she quite enjoyed the mood.

"To marry Justin Timberlake and move to LA," she finally answered just as I was about to start lecturing her.

I sucked my teeth and shook my head, raising myself off the floor to get my phone. When we first met, Nayana had tried to pressure me to join a sorority, but I could never understand what they were about.

How are they any different from cults in Nigerian universities? God forbid! That would no doubt be an opportunity to disgrace my parents.

She tried to get me initiated, and I tried to help her acquire some cultural sensibility. Her biggest setback was that she took great pride in her fluid American ways. The things she said sometimes convinced me that she needed to spend some time in Nigeria to shave some of her privilege.

I squinted as my eyes searched the room, patting my three-month-old braids.

"Girl, those braids are starting to decompose. They gotta go!" she hissed.

"Sharap, they still look good." I found my phone under a piece of cloth on the dresser. I pushed her to the other side of the bed and lay down facing the ceiling.

"Me, I just want to make my family proud. Unlike some people I know." I adjusted my pillow and checked if there were any new messages from Midowa.

"They teach y'all Nigerians to say that in school?" Nayana scoffed and turned over to press her phone, probably texting her silly boyfriend. There was nothing from Midowa, which meant that he was asleep. My thoughts carried me away to a place beyond the galaxy on my ceiling. I thought about Nayana's quip about my relationship being imaginary.

Of course she would say that because we're not a bunch of lustful teenagers like she and her foolish lover, I thought.

To me, Nayana was a walking contradiction of psychological paradigms. She was a person who, on the outside, looked like she knew herself but in reality was just lost. Her phone buzzed in her hand, and I heard the sound of her grin in the dark room.

"Hot mess!" she mumbled as she typed a reply. I imagined in that moment that it was me chatting with Midowa. *Does she even appreciate the simple privilege of being in the same time zone as her beloved, being able to text whenever she wanted without fear of waking him up or, worse, having to wait hours for a response?*

"Some people just need to go to Nigeria o," I said, talking to the ceiling and hoping that the dig would penetrate deep. I took every opportunity to work into conversations that she needed the experience to gain perspective on life. I enjoyed her company as a friend, but more than anything I felt responsible to train her. I had to be for her what Aunty Zubaida was for me. I hoped that every time she came to my house, she saw how I interacted with my parents, went about my chores, and overall conducted myself as a well-trained twenty-four-year-old.

"Tuh, when was the last time *you* went to Nigeria?" Nayana mocked.

"Ah, see you, me that would just fly now if I had the money. My father is waiting to have enough so that all of us will go and shake the town."

This was partly true. I had waited a long time for Dahdee to be able to afford for us to go to Nigeria because of my exorbitant tuition. At first it was because of papers, then money, and then, when both those things seemed not to be a problem, it appeared there was no longer the motivation to go. There was also the unspoken question of Aunty Zubaida's health, but her crises seemed to have come under some control that we wouldn't be risking a flare-up away from better health care. The idea that my parents would go somewhere for a while without Aunty Zubaida under their watch didn't seem likely.

"You, you don't have any excuse. Shey you people always travel for the holidays?" I retorted as usual. And as usual I reminded her how advantageous her American citizenship was for travel. It was a benefit that I had only recently come to have but had yet to fully enjoy. No one in the US seemed too impressed that I was an American citizen. I would have to leave these shores to mingle with people of lesser privilege for it to really mean something.

That was another thing Nayana had no appreciation for. She was born American, an identity that she did not have to run the qualification race for. The sacred blue passport was ready for her from birth as an American, paving the way to a coveted identity. I, on the other hand, had come to America through my father's lottery application. It took five years for us to be approved, but we appreciated the fact that we would be coming as permanent residents. We still had to meet certain conditions and jump through hoops to become eligible for citizenship. I lectured Nayana every chance I got about how easy she had it in life, never knowing what it's like to be an immigrant. Then again, I often thought of my friend Stella, who had spent four years without immigration status in Colorado after she finished undergrad. With three months to find a job, she could not meet the deadline and spent a year hiding from the public for fear of being deported. I almost resented Nayana for not knowing what any of that felt like.

Nayana lived about thirty minutes from me, and I remember the first time I met her parents at her house.

I practiced my smile behind her as we walked into their old stone-walled home.

"They can't wait to meet the Nigerian girl who is going to save their lost daughter," Nayana teased. I grinned internally, thinking that's exactly what was going to happen. As soon as her parents entered the living room, my petite body reached the floor in genuflection, my voice a high-pitched melody as I beamed at them like they were the president and first lady. Nayana teased me endlessly after that, saying that I transformed into an ingratiating house pet. I pitied her. She had no appreciation for the concept of parental reverence, which showed in the way she would casually greet my parents.

My phone vibrated, and I looked to see a message from my friend in New York, Stella. It was a long text telling me about a recent incident with her younger brother who was back home in Nigeria.

I started to tell Nayana about it, then decided not to. The context of the story would be very hard to verbalize to someone who couldn't appreciate how disturbing it is from a Nigerian standpoint. She would probably respond in simplistic words that would minimize the gravity of the disappointment I felt. Besides, I feared that sitting in the dark ambience was guaranteed to turn an already morbid subject into a dirge.

I fell asleep, the night sky overhead, with that thought in mind.

⁓⁓⁓⁓⁓

Saturday morning, I woke up at the edge of my bed while Nayana was sprawled out like an eagle. She was still sleeping, never the early riser between us two. I got out of bed and went to the balcony for some morning fresh air. I put a T-shirt over my nightgown and grabbed my iPod. Opening the screen door, I immediately felt the coolness overtake me.

The balcony welcomed me, and I hoped that Nayana would stay asleep for a while. This was my spot. With music in my ears, I would hang out here and watch the seasons change—summer to fall to winter and now the fading spring. Today was a good day to be out. The air was cool and refreshing, as it was a reminder that the early June days would soon usher in the heat. I was thankful for the chilly wind. Somehow my insides felt hotter than normal these days.

I always liked how close the trees were to our house, especially to my room. Their branches often leaned over so intimately, almost touching my screen door.

I rested my arms on the guardrail as I looked into the neighbour's' backyard, wondering if they too make time to enjoy the greenery. *Does the weather ever get this nice in Lagos?* I wondered. I didn't remember any such days when I was back home, but in the village there had been a lot of cool days during the harmattan season.

I suddenly didn't feel like putting on my earphones.

I shut my eyes and breathed in deeply, a faint whiff of magnolia catching my senses from the neighbour's lawn.

The trees had a vibrance to them. For me, they bloomed as a solid reminder that life is renewed after the frost of winter. I reread Stella's message. Her brother had an episode of madness, and her mother has been taking him from one prayer house to another hoping for a cure. The madness turned out to be a result of smoking weed and doing cocaine. They were looking into a rehab facility that was recommended by a family friend. My heart hurt for Stella. The first time I experienced Aunty Zubaida being hospitalized after a crisis, I felt like my heart had relocated to my intestines. I imagined Stella felt something like that.

My head swirled with questions. *What is Nigeria turning into?* In the Nigeria where I grew up, drugs existed only in the movies or in the form of kids fooling around with talcum powder. Occasionally there had been the odd, disgraceful story of a son or daughter of somebody who was deported from abroad for doing drugs. That son or daughter would then become the object of children's satire, where they mimicked a drug addict's behaviour as seen on TV. Stella's brother was a good kid. *How did he get mixed up with such rubbish?*

I sucked in a full breath to cleanse my thoughts. I decided I would call Stella later. I turned on some music to distract my brain from the tragedy. I eventually went back into the room, and the sound of my slippers flip-flopping finally woke Nayana.

"Good morning, Madam President," I greeted her in a thick Nigerian accent, folding clothes from the laundry basket. "Oya, come. Let's go make breakfast, abi do you want it in bed?" Nayana kicked the covers and pulled herself up to a long stretch, pretending not to hear me. "You cannot say good morning, ehn?" I continued, picking up a pillow from the bed and throwing it at her.

"Gosh, it's only eight o'clock," Nayana moaned, looking at her phone.

"See you, by this time your mates are already in the farm working hard."

We finally headed downstairs after Nayana realized there would be no peace for her in bed.

I showed her how to make pancakes the Nigerian way, with scrambled eggs, and served my parents in the living room, where they ate while watching the news. Nayana and I settled down at the dining table and compared households. Nayana talked about how annoying her two younger brothers were and how they would eat everything in their path. To me, it was a privilege to have siblings. I often reminisced about the ways I used to annoy Aunty Zubaida.

The cool air from the window carried the shrieks of the neighbour's kids in the yard. After breakfast we remained at the dining table, me with my laptop and Nayana scrolling endlessly through Facebook. I found limited information on alternatives to restraints, but words like *trauma* and *unsafe* jumped out at me. When I felt my scatterbrain being overloaded, I looked up to start a conversation with Nayana, who did not want to be bothered.

"Naya?" She lowered her cell phone, frowning at the near-whisper of her name.

"Yes?" she responded, waiting for me to speak. My eyes were still fixed on the laptop for a few minutes before I finally looked up.

"What if one of your siblings was disabled. How would you feel?" I raised my head slowly and stared at her. Nayana shifted in her chair, looking startled by the question.

"What do you mean?"

"Like what if Mabo or Tobi was autistic or had some type of delay. How would you feel?"

"Is that a trick question? How would anyone feel?" She continued frowning.

"I just feel badly for these kids at the centre but I also think of their family members like how do they cope?."

"I mean, I guess you just deal with it, right? My friend's brother is autistic, and they seem fine."

I scoffed and put my feet up on the adjacent chair. "It's interesting because in Nigeria, when you say someone is disabled, it means there's a physical handicap, so everyone can see it and they can empathize or whatever, but when it comes to cognitive or mental disabilities, eemm, it's hard to explain to people there."

"So they don't get autism?"

"Eeemm, not that they don't get it. I mean, they see the symptoms, but their concept of it is usually more of personal responsibility or just a spiritual problem. Take, for instance, a child who is doing poorly in school. Here they would go through some kind of test and then be diagnosed as having a learning disability, right? In Nigeria, that's a foreign concept. The child would simply be tagged as dim-witted or as an underachiever, so the solution is to just sit up and work harder. You see what I mean?"

Nayana nodded slowly.

"So what do they do for people with the 'physical' disabilities they know of?" she asked, signing air quotes.

"There are still programs to help them, but it's really hard to get over the superstitions and stigmas that people have about such things. Honestly, if you can hide it, the better for you. Which is why I sometimes wonder if it's really a good idea to even diagnose these learning disabilities in children, because when you think about the label, you can see how it would be easier for a child to thrive believing that they just need to work harder as opposed to the oh-I -have-a-disability mindset. You get?" I sighed, watching the frown on Nayana's face.

"So you don't think kids should be diagnosed?"

"Not—"

Nayana cut in. "Because you realize the purpose of the diagnosis is to give the child a chance to qualify for additional services that will then help them learn in a way that is tailored to their needs, right? I think you're looking at it the wrong way."

I sighed heavily. Nayana was still so far removed from Nigerian culture that she could never understand what I was trying to say.

"No, you're right. I mean, this is my field, right, so yeah, I hear you. Sometimes I just wonder about the other side of it, you know. Like everything else, there are pros and cons."

"Of course, but better to have services than not, right? Look at your aunt. She would qualify for disability based on her sickle cell if, say, she couldn't work or just needed some additional services. So wouldn't you rather she had access to it than be stuck because of her illness?"

"Yeah. I get what you're saying. It's just hard sometimes to come to terms with the fact that even though I've lived here for some time now, it's still new to me. So yeah, if my aunt were to get on disability, someone from back home would think in terms of a handicap and ask, 'Is she disabled?' To them, she's not disabled; she's just sick. It doesn't carry the same stigma. It's just a different concept—disability—which I get makes sense here when you think in terms of services."

Muhmee walked into the kitchen, her flip-flops dragging under the weight of her slender, petite body. "My dear, are you okay?" she asked Nayana.

"Yes, thanks, Aunty," she responded.

"Muhmee, thank you," I added, referring to breakfast.

"Ehen, my dear. What are you girls going to do today?"

"Nothing oo. We'll just chill and then she'll be going back home this evening," I said, pointing in Nayana's direction.

"Okay then. If I don't see you before you go, please greet your parents for me, all right?"

"Yes, Aunty."

"Samira, the dishes, ok" Muhmee said and walked out.

Chapter 4

SOUL-SEARCHING

I still had a lot of conflict in my head around the subject of mental health and disability in Nigeria. A recurring thought I had was the old saying that what a culture has no language for does not exist in that culture. I couldn't help wondering if perhaps the introduction of drugs into Nigerian media contributed to the growing problem. I needed to get Dahdee's opinion on the matter, so when Nayana wanted to retire to the room for some mindless Facebook scrolling, I convinced her to come hang out with Dahdee.

Dahdee was watching football on ESPN and looked pleased that we were joining him. I realized in that moment how much adult life had changed the dynamics between us. Dahdee had introduced me to the sport, and we used to watch games together throughout my childhood. Some of my favourite memories included sitting in a corner a safe distance from the adults, including Dahdee and his male friends, all of their booming voices shouting over one another as they ran commentary on the game. My eyes would be blinking so fast as I searched the screen for some observation I could point out to

Dahdee for his approval. I'd drop a pearl about a player's move, and he would beam at me, confirming to his friends that his daughter was surely on the right path, with the right team.

"The other clubs are not worth our time!" Dahdee would say, and I would nod like a bona fide protégé. So it goes. The fans of a football club know as part of the rules that no matter what ranking their club had, loyalty was the prime thing. As far as the sell went, Arsenal had been having a good run of winning trophies for the past five years. Their games were a thrill to watch as the players demonstrated discipline and raw skill, in addition to the fact that they had the legendary Kanu Nwankwo playing for them.

As life got busier and I got further into my own head, I passed up opportunities to watch the game with Dahdee. I wondered if he missed that too and if that was why he still insisted on dashing me money at random. Perhaps that was his way of reminding me that I would never be too old to be daddy's girl.

I fried up some prawn crackers that Dahdee always brought back from his trips to New York. I saved some to lure Aunty Zubaida to visit, as always. We would reminisce about the good old days back in Nigeria when we peered into the pot as the transparent plate transformed with a dance into the white crispy goodness.

"Thank you, my dear," Dahdee said as I served him the crackers with a glass of juice.

I settled onto the couch beside Nayana and set the snack between us.

"Hmm, Fenerbace and Man U, that's serious o," I commented on the sports teams as the crackers popped in my mouth.

"Don't mind these boys. I don't even know what they're doing." He waved his hand dismissively and sipped his juice.

"Dahdee, Nayana and I were talking about something, and we wanted to get your input," I started.

"Go ahead." He turned down the TV volume and shifted in my direction.

"Have you heard of rehabs in Nigeria? Like for drugs?"

"Eeem, yes, I've heard of one. Somebody was telling me recently they are now popping up."

"That's what I heard o, Dahdee. So what do you think of that?"

"Well, obviously it's becoming more of a problem, so it's a welcome development. It just worries me that things are trending in that direction. But it's the price of westernization, I guess."

I nodded. "Hmm, seems like we're quicker to adopt the bad behaviours than anything useful."

Dahdee chuckled and dusted his hands of the crumbs. "There have been many positive influences, and the westerners also borrow from us, but you're right that it would be better if we take the good and leave the bad."

"Yeah, like mental health. We still have some catching up to do."

"Well, yes, but you have to understand that we Nigerians are a strong-willed people. The level of endurance in our collective existence shapes our character so much so that resilience is the prescribed medication for any adversity. So it has desensitized us in a way that we see it as something to pray about instead of thinking up solutions."

I looked at Nayana to make sure she was paying attention. Dahdee was speaking deep facts. The reactions to events that disrupt psychological balance were very different between the Western and the traditional societies. I thought about my aunt, who was locked away for some unknown mental issue until she died. I struggled with the thought that Dahdee let it happen; he certainly knew about it. With his exposure and education, he could have advocated for her to get professional help. Perhaps he tried. I knew of cases where people had sent money and set up care for their loved one, but the ignorant family members continued their unsavoury practices.

"Okay, Dahdee, but where are we with diplomacy in getting aid for mental health?" I loved to use big words in conversation with my parents. It was a way to show them that the school fees they paid had not gone to waste.

"Ah, my dear, have they finished collecting aid for other bigger issues concerning health? Look at HIV, sickle cell, even our common malaria. Those are more of a priority; meanwhile, if you're talking about funds, Nigeria has all the money it needs, but if you mean aid as in policies and brains, well . . ." He chuckled and shook his head.

He continued. "Okay, just think of this. My friend who had an accident is now in a wheelchair, but he gets around just fine, as every building he goes into is wheelchair accessible. Just imagine what his life would have been like if he was in Nigeria. Just a few buildings have elevators that sometimes don't even work. Let them even construct ramps for a start so that wheelchairs can go up instead of struggling with stairs. You see the point?"

I nodded. I did see the point: There was yet a lot of work to be done. Accessibility was something that really impressed me when I came to the States. I noticed how older people were still out and about, taking the bus with their walkers, electric scooters, and electric wheelchairs. They could still get on the bus because the driver would collapse some seats, and with the push of a button, a steel ramp would descend with a whirring sound, and the passenger would ride on up, unimpressed by the amazing technology. People's disabilities and handicaps were factored into policies and planning in this government. Charles Darwin may have had Nigeria in mind when he spoke of survival of the fittest. The expectation was that those with any kind of handicap were to be left at home while the others picked up the struggle.

Nayana exclaimed at times as the conversation continued, commenting on how sad it must be to live in Nigeria, much to my annoyance.

"I remember once when I interviewed a pastor on my radio show," Dahdee continued, and I shifted in my seat, glancing at Nayana and hoping she was taking note of how cool my father was to have been on the radio. "He spoke about the work they do to help the community and the challenges they sometimes face. I asked him about the availability of services for the deaf and blind, and he was just giving excuses about their ignorance, but at least to his credit, he accepted responsibility. This was what got me. He told stories of churches in the past where they had found some strange-looking documents that seemed useless and turned them into waste paper for selling akara—you know akara, right?" he asked Nayana.

"I've heard of it, yeah," she responded dryly.

"Good. It's a fried bean pastry sold on the streets, very greasy. So it turns out that this akara paper was actually braille that the colonial masters had left behind for the blind. Imagine that! Whether they didn't know what it was or they just didn't care, that was how they wasted them."

"So lack of education is the problem then?" I asked.

"Ehn, lack of education but also lack of sensitivity to the importance of services for ones with disabilities. Look at the government budget. How much of it goes towards programs for disability or mental health in Nigeria? Not enough, so funding is important. And the public needs to be sensitized to the value of such programs because, see, you can bring in all the aid you want to Nigeria, but the people will still squander it because they don't see the value. Suffering and smiling is our culture. To a Nigerian, anything beyond the normal day-to-day life survivability is a luxury. For a government that has not even been able to ensure steady power for its citizens, why do they care that something is wrong with your mental health? A shot of hot traditional gin or a few strokes of the cane for a child would set them straight."

I chuckled. That was certainly what we were taught to believe—that a person could overcome mental problems with enough tough love. And don't even think of harming yourself in the name of distress. That would surely reveal a lack of gratitude and trust in the power of God.

One day when I was about eight years old, I heard Muhmee panic on a phone call. Her friend Aunty Toyin was in the hospital. She had been found in her apartment, alone and on the floor. Somebody had apparently noticed that she hadn't been taking phone calls, perhaps a family member, and went to check on her.

I followed Muhmee to the hospital. We checked in with the nurses who sauntered about like they had more important places to be.

When we walked into Aunty Toyin's room, I instantly knew that something was different about this visit. I had gone with Muhmee on many occasions to visit a sick person, and the air of sympathy was typically palpable with all the *heya* and other laments.

This one felt like we were treading on a path where thieves were known to be lurking, pretending to be unfazed while remaining hypervigilant and ready to run or surrender. Muhmee had taken on a pretentious air of casualness that was so uncharacteristic of her, making random comments about how she had run into people we knew. In her defence this was after the usual question of *How are you feeling?* and other prompts that a sick person would normally respond to yielded nothing.

Aunty Toyin did not utter a word, not even as much as a sound for the whole hour and a half we were there. She simply stared through blank eyes—blank with a hint of condemnation. With her hand under her chin, she made only a slight adjustment in her torso but remained still, her head propped up on a pillow. She blinked sluggishly, in no hurry to respond or even to disengage. She kept her eyes fixed on Muhmee and me with her hand covering her mouth, perhaps hiding words that she may have been speaking to herself.

It was only when I whispered to Muhmee that I was hungry that we finally got up to leave. Muhmee said goodbye to Aunty Toyin, promising that she would pray hard for her and thus she would be well. On the car ride home, I had feared that I would get yelled at for interrupting a very important visit, but Muhmee raised no objection. In fact, I suspected, judging by the way that she had repeated *hungry* out loud in such an exaggerated tone of voice, that it was a welcome exit strategy. The visit had been too heavy even for Muhmee.

"Muhmee, what happened to Aunty Toyin?" I had asked on the way home.

"My dear, hmm." She sighed heavily. "It's just the work of the devil, honestly."

Muhmee had launched into speculation that somebody may have bewitched her. That made sense because, otherwise, how would

Aunty Toyin, who was normally jovial and talkative, be staring like that and not saying a word? *How unfortunate*, I thought. I really liked Aunty Toyin. She always called me smart and aware for my age.

It was only later in life that the story became clearer—that Aunty Toyin's soon-to-be husband jilted her without any reason, causing a mental breakdown. There may have even been an attempt to take her life, at the very least a passive death wish by starvation.

It was a proper disaster. Aunty Toyin was thirty-seven, and I knew so well how diligently she had tried to find a husband, trying to outrun the old maiden syndrome. At her age she was fast decaying, and she needed to settle down quickly. I myself had wished a good husband upon her, thinking how much she deserved one. Growing up in a world where women spend their lives racing against their biological clocks, I learned as a child to commiserate with the unmarried ones at a young age, verbalizing hope for them.

"Ehh, Aunty, see your fine face but no husband? I will pray for you, and husband will come!" Muhmee said I once told a customer in her shop when I was five years old.

I knew I wouldn't be married in my twenties. Honestly, I hardly pictured myself being married at all, and if I ever did, I would be at least thirty-five. I was caught between the path of my grandmother and my mum, the former who never married. I hardly ever spoke these thoughts out loud, especially when I was in Nigeria. As far as people were concerned, I was just as eager as they were to find me a husband. That was tradition; nobody cared about your own personal ideals.

Still, Aunty Toyin's plight had struck me as valid. There was a real and raw misery that the Nigerian society was waiting to impose on you when you pass a marriageable age. Yet, as valid as her tragedy was, I never stopped thinking all those years that the idea of taking her life would have been overreacting. People just don't do such things in Nigeria.

Hours later, Nayana and I retired to my room, ears still ringing with Dahdee's concluding thought: a single stick cannot sweep the whole house; you need a broom.

"But you sef, Aunty Zubaida. You know Mummy doesn't like this," I confronted my incorrigible aunt on the phone about her relationship with a married man.

I looked around the city bus as people gave me uncomfortable looks and tried to lower my voice. I was on my way to the centre a week later and hoped that the next connection would be on time so that I could be there at eight o'clock sharp.

"See, smallie, my break will soon be over. If you don't have anything else to say, lemme go." Aunty Zubaida was the only person allowed to call me smallie, even though she wasn't that much taller than me. Midowa knew it was reserved for Aunty Zubaida but would keep trying it on every chance he got.

"Na wa o, Aunty Zubaida. What are you doing at work on a Saturday?" At first when she newly got the job, she would volunteer for weekend shifts to make a good impression. After a year of being there, I couldn't understand why she was still making the sacrifice.

"I don't understand. You go pay my bills?" She scoffed.

"Okay o." I paused. "Shey you'll still braid my hair next week?"

"Bye-bye, jor." I heard the phone click.

Aunty Zubaida's no-nonsense approach startled people who didn't know her. I did, and even though I wished she was nicer, I didn't let it intimidate me. She was not afraid to confront anybody in life and would tell me I tried too hard to please people and needed to grow a backbone.

"See, smallie, with this your size and your baby face, people will just intimidate you if you're too nice. You need to show them small crase." But I had more sense than that. What she called being a people pleaser I called having a conscience. Really, how could she, somebody who is dating a married man, be giving advice?

As much as I didn't approve of Aunty Zubaida's mischievousness, I found it fascinating and, oddly enough, reassuring. Nothing in life seemed to ruffle her, especially not her health condition. It was like she did not even believe it existed. Meanwhile, I wondered constantly if she would live long. Nothing stopped her from doing what she wanted to do at the time, certainly not previous mistakes. Every experience to her was new, and she would give it her all with the mindset that if it failed, she would simply start over.

Perhaps I found that comforting because it was better to see her in control than to witness her state of helplessness and surrender to pain.

I couldn't deny that I was a bit jealous of Aunty Zubaida. She was easily attractive, with a face like Muhmee's, only a little more refined. She was sought after by most men who came across her. She was about a head taller than me and always teased me for being the smallie. As a child I wanted so badly to someday grow as tall as Aunty Zubaida, but as time went on, I realized that I would never be able to look at Zubaida eye to eye. Not that she would have let that happen even if I had the height. Aunty Zubaida was only five years older than me, but by cultural ramifications, that put her in aunty category. Therefore, the title, while appropriate because she was in fact my aunt, was really more in reference to the power differential between us. Zubaida sometimes threatened to beat me up when she was annoyed. I would then straighten up because I knew the beating would be worth her while. Thankfully, she never laid a hand on me, and I really did not ever try to test the threat.

I knew too well that my aunty's beauty was her very undoing. I didn't really think as a child that she was pretty, but the fact that she was constantly getting compliments made me realize it was a good thing that I looked like her. As I got older, I hoped that I would use this beauty in much less destructive ways. I had skin the colour of butterscotch like my dad, only I was a shade darker. Grandma on Dahdee's side was light skinned, a sharp contrast to Muhmee's side. Muhmee was an ebony black beauty and so was Aunty Zubaida. With velvety dark skin shining like tar, Aunty Zubaida seemed to evade the characteristic paleness of sickle cell anaemia. Only the dull yellow pupils of her small eyes were a telltale sign. Still, she watched the world like a curious bird and gave no consideration to being anything but authentically herself. That night she first came to our house, she had examined me with those bird eyes, and I had stared right back in stark curiosity, both of us unaware that we would henceforth become sisters.

My parents and I were outside in the building compound when an uncle walked up the stairs with a young girl following him who looked about twelve. He exchanged pleasantries with Muhmee and Dahdee and suddenly had to rush off. He left the young girl standing there with her Ghana-must-go bag filled with whatever possessions she had deemed essential. Muhmee had spent a quick minute assessing the girl to see if she was okay and then rustled her into our flat, with me shadowing her. There was never any formal explanation to me as to why Aunty Zubaida, whom I recognized from visiting Grandma, had come to visit and how long she would be staying. It wasn't a problem for me; I didn't mind the company. As long as she did not try to become the centre of attention for however many days she would be staying.

Days turned into months and then into years, and just like that Aunty Zubaida became my older sister, leaving behind her mother, the infamous Ufendo, in Kano.

I often wondered what the women on Dahdee's side of the family were like. Perhaps I was more like them. Muhmee's side had too many scandalous behaviours—Grandma, who freed herself of the baggage of her child; Aunty Zubaida, who lived fast with men; Muhmee . . .

Well, not me. Thanks to Aunty Zubaida, I learned early on in life that my role was to be the good girl. I loved education and thrived on my parents' praise.

"Oh yes, she is such an intelligent girl." I glowed when my parents bragged to their friends. It didn't matter that I didn't believe it; it was only important that they did. But that was only half the battle. I also had to be morally responsible.

Aunty Zubaida did well enough in university but was inevitably distracted by her wayward behaviour. I had been an accomplice in many escapades, where some man on the street wanted to get her attention. It was no secret that she loved her men, as she would go with anyone who had the right funds to shower on her. She didn't care much for the fine boys. She wanted a life where she would have the nicest of things. Money looked good on her beauty, she would say, and complimented it in the best way.

"These UNILAG people will see something special. They don't know me yet!" she would brag at night-time when we gisted, her beautiful egusi seed-shaped eyes gleaming in anticipation.

I would gulp in every word and excitedly pulled out all the details of my aunty's plan to take down Nigeria's most socially acclaimed university. She promised me protection, and I knew for sure that she would be every bit as popular as she claimed and that I would be too, at least by association. That didn't appeal to me. I pictured all kinds of dangerous scenarios where we would get into some kind of scandal that would ruin both our lives. Besides, I had planned to apply to the renowned University of Ife, where the field of psychology was well established. That was the school that would adequately train me to become a psych guru with a successful practice somewhere in Lagos. Unless, of course, Dahdee came and whisked me away to America.

As my final year approached, I spent nights praying that our visas would come through in time for university. To go to school in America would put my pedigree on a whole new level.

When we finally made it to the States, I was determined to be the child my parents expected me to be. I did things in full cognizance of how it would reflect on me before my parents and in turn on my parents before the large community in Nigeria and the small community abroad. Sure, I had made mistakes that almost shattered my good record, but I retraced my steps and guaranteed that they never happened again. Yet the shadow that grew with me from childhood, the twisted history of these female figures in my life, loomed.

How could I possibly outrun that shadow?

Chapter 5

SAVIOUR COMPLEX

I stumbled through the door at 7:59 a.m. and enthusiastically greeted Ms. Rhonda.

Usually I worked on weekdays and sometimes in the evening to help with night routines after school. That day, our centre was hosting a panel discussion titled "Adults Living with Autism," and Ms. Rhonda had asked us to prepare the kids for the event. The presenters had travelled all over the country visiting centres for autism as well as other schools to share their struggles and triumphs living with the diagnosis.

I spotted Dorcy in the common room rocking back and forth, pressing his fingers together like he was moulding Play-Doh. As usual, he opened his mouth wide like he was about to yawn, and then all of a sudden, his face collapsed again into a blank stare. He was not a disruptive kid and was often the calm in the storm when other kids were going off. When provoked, however, he quickly transformed into a raging storm of profanities, hitting himself on the head and crying inconsolably. I prayed that morning, as I always did, that we would have an uneventful day. My body didn't feel like doing restraints, and quite frankly, I didn't want to ruin the nice blouse I had put on for the event.

"Good morning, ma'am." I avoided Ms. Rhonda's keen eyes so that she wouldn't notice mine were puffy from staying up late to watch Nollywood movies on YouTube.

She was an interesting woman, Ms. Rhonda.

She was a small, burly figure with enough confidence to convince me that Muhmee was right when she said that big things come in small packages. My co-workers seemed to always have a problem with her. She was quick to correct and quick to direct but never too involved in anything. She seemed to always transcend the excitement of the kids going off or the staff running amok.

She sometimes brought two boys in with her from one of the sister schools.

I always greeted her, and we would chat briefly. It didn't take long before she asked where I'm originally from. She shared stories about Africans she knew and asked if my family and I were connected to any of the African associations and why not. She was kind, but I got the feeling that I would not want to get on her bad side.

There were other things I could have been doing that day, but when Ms. Rhonda asked if I could come in, I couldn't say no. After Dorcy finished his breakfast of a peanut butter sandwich, I helped him put away his dishes, showing him the proper placements. We went into his room, where I helped him straighten things up and grab a few items he might need for the event. It was already 8:45 a.m., and the event was starting in about an hour. I took Dorcy outside to get some fresh air before heading to the event hall behind the housing quarters.

Outside, we sat in the playground enjoying the greenery and the enveloping June heat. I picked up a daffodil from the grass and watched Dorcy as he paced the grounds, chanting at intervals. Occasionally he would look my way with his usual blank stare. Even after three months, his eyes did not register any recognition.

"Brodur! Brodurrrrr!" I had gotten used to the chant that at first sounded nonsensical.

At least I got a kid who was verbal. Some of the others did not speak but would only grunt and laugh out loud. As I spent more time with him, I floated between fearing his outbursts and learning how to manage his triggers.

The first week I was assigned to him, I spent hours trying to figure out what he wanted. Until Ms. Rhonda pulled me aside weeks later to tell me he really was saying *brother*. He was calling out to his younger brother who had died in a car accident.

"Hey, buddy!" I picked up his palm to touch mine in a lazy high five. "Time to go."

"Brodurrrr," he continued as I guided him by the elbow towards the hall.

We gathered the children into the conference hall, each one accompanied by their own aide, who prompted them to maintain good behaviour. There were three men and two women visiting, from the high functioning to the more socially impaired on the autism spectrum. The guest speakers all introduced themselves and talked about their experiences with stigma and their family's creative ways of supporting them.

When it came time for questions, I raised my hand. My question was directed to a woman whose remarkable wit and spirited defence of her diagnosis gave me something to think about.

"Hi, thank you so much for sharing your experience and rec-ommendations for our program. My question to you is regarding the correct term to describe a person who has been diagnosed with autism. What do you think is appropriate versus offensive?"

"That's a good question," she responded, her voice strong and confident, with a hint of robotic rigidity. "Personally, I think it's okay to say 'autistic'; it doesn't bother me. I think you can always tell when someone is prejudiced from the way they treat you."

Ms. Rhonda spoke into her microphone.

"I appreciate your answer, Ms. Ferret. We at the centre believe in person-first language, so we teach our staff to say 'person living with autism' as opposed to 'autistic.'"

"You can say whatever you want, but to me that just sounds like a mouthful. I mean, I call myself autistic, and it doesn't change who I am. It has no more meaning than I allow it to."

I heard the soft gasps from my colleagues and lowered my head to hide any reaction to that takedown of the supervisor. That spitfire woman was not going to be told how to interpret her own experience.

I glanced at Dorcy's face throughout the event and imagined what was going through his mind and if he had any takeaways from all that was said. In his internal world, were there dreams? Did he have friends? Did he *want* friends? What wish would he want granted if given the opportunity? I tried many times before to ask these questions and draw him into conversation. I ended up in dialogue with myself about how awful it would be to lose a sibling and not even be able to understand the implication of it. I processed it with Midowa later that evening, trying to explain why Dorcy was so low functioning.

"Na wa o, so what will cure him?" he asked, half yawning. "What exactly is the treatment for this autism thing sef?" We had exchanged countless messages about autism in my school days, and I was slightly annoyed that he would still ask that. I expected him to know better.

"Eeem, there is no particular treatment as far as I know. I guess it depends on where somebody is on the spectrum and then it comes down to managing the behavioural issues."

"You say?" I rolled my eyes, hearing the sarcasm in his voice.

"Think of it as a scale of numbers that increases from mild symptoms to severe. Some people will have only some unusual be-haviours, like not wanting to be touched or being obsessed with routine. The ones further down will have more severe problems, like language delay, high sensitivity to sounds and touch, and repetitive movements. The goal is to tackle the specific behaviours depending on the outcome you are hoping for."

"So the boy is on the severe end?" he asked.

"Yes, although a few other kids have it worse than him sef. At least he can talk."

"Kai, this world sef. Ehn, so many things wrong with people, especially these poor children."

"My dear, na so oo."

"It's good sha. It's nice people like you who can do this work," he said.

Nice people like me.

I certainly thought that of the people I worked with, especially my supervisor. They had genuine empathy for those with developmental disabilities and committed their life to supporting them. I wasn't sure that I fit into that category of really understanding the work involved and being moved purely by empathy.

Case in point: There used to be a boy at our neighbour's house. I liked playing with his sister but was always afraid to go to their house. I remember the dingy feel of the house when the boy would stagger into the living room, growling as his giant feet scraped the floor, drooling all over his six-foot frame. I used to tense up when he came into the same room as me, and his mum would assure me that he was harmless. I still felt like bolting through the door. That house used to give me the creeps. Because of the boy, it seemed to take on an especially frightening atmosphere, like darkness was always looming over it. It felt like a dungeon where a hungry monster lived and I was the prey. I never believed his family's assurance that he wouldn't hurt me. I just knew that if he ever attacked anyone, it would be me, like a dog that goes after the person who smelled of fear and distrust. Eventually I stopped going there to spare his mother the embarrassment of constantly trying to pacify me.

No one knew that story, about how I used to fear people like that kid whose behaviours were more than just weird. I was too ashamed to tell anyone, even Midowa, and so when he called me nice, I responded modestly, "My dear, we all have to try."

I had just gotten to the point where I could recognize spectrum behaviours and fake competence in dealing with people like that neighbour kid. Yet the so-called impostor syndrome haunted me every day, even though I schooled Midowa every chance I got, pretending to be an expert. I wondered if the people I worked with could see through me. They would rattle off clinical terms and speak so eloquently about the underpinnings of behaviours that would seem odd to an inexperienced person. I wanted more than anything to sound like them, to tap into their vocabulary and use politically correct and inoffensive language.

"Anyway," I said, changing the subject. "So, at the seminar, one of the speakers was saying that it's okay to say 'autistic,' but Rhonda was like, no, we say 'person living with autism.' Omo, it was such a treat to see that interaction. Nobody questions Rhonda o, but she met her match!"

"So what's your opinion?" Midowa asked, his voice heavy with sleep. The time on my phone said 8:00 p.m., which meant it was about 2:00 a.m. for him.

"Rhonda was right—language is very important. And I agree that it should focus on the person more than the diagno—"

Midowa cut in. "Ehn, but I also see the woman's point. It's like somebody saying 'girl who is Black' instead of 'Black girl.'"

"Well, that's different, but I don't know, jor. Sometimes in this country, I think people are just too sensitive. There is always a chance that you will offend them."

"Wait—you call your supervisor by her name?" Midowa asked.

"Yeah. She asked me to." I was not in the mood to convince him that I hadn't lost my good home training. "Something I found really interesting was one other woman shared her experience of being diagnosed when her daughter got her own diagnosis. I was surprised. An adult realizing that the struggles she has had in her life were because she had autism; meanwhile, it was revealed only while she was focusing on her nine-year-old daughter's issues."

"Ha, so how was she able to take care of her child?"

I paused at that question, wanting to reply something sarcastic like, *What, she cannot take care of her child because she's autistic?* But then I thought honestly about my own reaction as I listened to the woman speak. I was struck by the fact that right next to her on the panel was a man who presented with the classic autism behaviours, and it was a stark image of the diversity in the spectrum of autism. The woman shared incidents where she would be having meltdowns when she had to make choices, and the awkwardness of not being able to hug or enjoy physical touch. When she got the diagnosis, she was relieved to know that contrary to what some people thought, she was neither crazy nor stone cold. Then again, she was also worried about having to live with this new label for the rest of her life. Though, to be honest, how she was able to parent her child had come up in my mind. I wondered, if she had been diagnosed in childhood like her daughter, could that label have caused her and the people in her life to limit her to the point where she would not be the mother of four children that she became? I couldn't blame Midowa for asking that question. I only happened to know better because of my exposure in the field.

My phone beeped, and the call went dead. I tried to call back but heard that my call credit had been exhausted. I started typing in the BBM chat, and a message from Midowa came in saying he was trying to call back but it wouldn't connect.

Maybe network, I typed. Let's just chat.

I picked up where we'd left off. So she sounded like a good parent, and she said it was when her daughter's clinician asked her questions about her child that she started to wonder about herself and decided to get an assessment. That's how she found out o that she was on the spectrum. I waited to see if he was starting to type.

I continued, knowing it wouldn't be much longer before he would doze off. She now said something about how people forget that children with autism have their own unique personality that develops as they grow and things change. It made me think of my aunty and how they said she behaved as a child and then when she got older.

Midowa did not approve of my conclusion that my late aunt may have had autism, but he knew better than to say that.

Hmm, na wa oo, so basically there may be adults here who we know of that are autistic. His messages were slow coming in.

You know what would be better? If you say "on the spectrum" instead of "autistic."

Haa, that one will be confusing, nau. People will be wondering what spectrum I'm talking about.

Ehn, say "autism spectrum." I'm just telling you what my supervisor told me.

Ah, okay ooo. Hmm, me, I thought the autism thing was for kids sha?

Kids eventually become adults, right?

That's true, mehn. I don't just understand all these things.

I don't think anyone really does. We're all just trying to make sense of it.

After a brief pause, we both noticed that the conversation was stalling.

Do you know you're changing? Midowa typed.

Hian, how?

You're becoming Americanized.

As per the way I talk or what? Whenever we spoke on the phone I did sound more nasal than usual and made my *r* sounds a little harder. Other than that, I didn't think that in regular speech my accent had changed that much. Waiting for his reply, I contemplated the meaning of what he said. It was not the first time someone back home had said me, "Hmm, you're changing o," like it's a thing to be ashamed of. I was constantly pulled in opposite directions, trying to reconcile the two worlds that now shaped my identity. When I first came to this country, I was advised by teachers and concerned acquaintances alike to adapt quickly. No, not adapt but to strip off that Africanness that would stereotype me. I needed to mimic my classmates' accents to avoid the blank stares and interruptions asking me to repeat what I said because they couldn't understand my jungle language. I had to swap *wotah* for *waterrr* if I wanted to blend in. Even in writing class papers, I had to drop the *u* from words like *neighbour* and *odour* if I did not want points docked from my work.

Midowa had laughed at me for spelling the word *colour* without the *u*, and I had to explain the concept of American English to him. I suspected that he was not satisfied and that he somehow expected me to defy this new norm for authenticity. He had no idea the cost if I were to insist on sounding the same way when I was speaking publicly or holding on to the limited ideas I had coming to America.

Just the things that you are occupied with these days, all these oyibo tins, he answered.

Has it ever occurred to you that I'm now grown-up? I hoped he felt the caustic bite of those words, ready for the fight.

When he took too long to respond, I added: Besides, I'm talking about things that concern my profession, things that are important to people who have to deal with this every day of their lives. hat's wrong with that? Is it a bad thing to learn? Or to change the way you used to think based on new things that you've experienced or even talk about those things to educate other people? This is the kind of mentality that holds us back as Nigerians. Instead of applying new information to solve problems, we criticize people who dare to explore and allow themselves to embrace a paradigm shift.

I pushed hard on the send button, feeling my breath quicken and my heart beat faster. Midowa would have to look up the word *paradigm*, much to my tasty delight. I couldn't wait to use that term after hearing professors and classmates over use it throughout undergrad. At first I read it as *paradig-um* until I heard them finish it off with a *dime*". It was such a powerful word, the kind that would roll off the tongue of Nigerian politicians as they shuffled through their pack of lies. It was a word that would come to challenge my core beliefs and expose an inherent stubbornness in my heritage. So if Midowa was somehow suggesting that I was posing, then he could chew on that.

Calm down, ahnahn. I was just pointing it out I didn't say it's bad. After all, when in Rome, act like the Romans, right? he responded.

Right. No wahala lemme go and finish my chores," I typed, disappointed with that conclusion. He had not even acknowledged my point—the fact that I was growing into a woman and naturally changing. He would never understand the untold battle that immigrants have to fight, a burden to remain the same for your people, frozen in time so as not to disrupt their narrative of who you are, the exact same person who left home. Meanwhile, your new home pulls at your old clothes, dragging them off you and forcing on a new awareness, one that knows new and advanced things much too cool to be kept quiet. So, in the end, who you are is somewhere between fitting in and staying the same. Seeing that there is no perfect balance between the two, the exhausting choice left is to decide who you would be more comfortable disappointing.

I said a tired good night and started to pick at my baby hairs, thinking how unlikely that he and I will ever be able to fully reconcile our worlds and get back the connection that we had in the beginning.

Midowa and I had flirted for a while in secondary school before we even knew we liked each other. I never wanted to be the one to profess love, so I waited to see what Midowa would do. That was until the Law happened.

There was the school celebrity, and he was notoriously called the Law. And he was *a* law all to himself. Lawrence had but one objective in the school—to break hearts and hold girls hostage, swooning at the mercy of his charm.

We were all in the exam hall, writing physics, and I still had some questions to answer. Lawrence for whatever reason, Lawrence was staring at me from the adjacent part of the room. He had been sitting a few rows in front and kept turning back to look at me, that mischievous smile plastered on his face. It seemed like the crowded exam hall was the perfect place to practice his newfound antics. It just made everything all the more interesting; perhaps it was a distraction for those who were so gifted that they were easily bored by the questions and in the same vein a distraction for those who were so heartbroken over the questions that they couldn't answer. Lawrence belonged in the latter group, as brain matter was not necessarily his strong suit. The principal didn't call him NFA—no future ambition—as she did many of the boys because his charm was irresistible. NFA was how she qualified boys whom she projected would not amount to much and whom she wanted her best girls to stay away from. Even to the teachers he was a favourite. They would grade his work with pity, imploring him to make something of himself academically and cajoling him to think about how much of a success he would be if he did.

Lawrence stood up from where he was seated and dusted off his pants in full display of all the other students in the room. His broad shoulders spread wide, he sauntered out of the room but not before accidentally throwing his pen right at my feet. I was the first one on the row of seats and eyed him suspiciously as he bent over to pick it up. When he raised himself, he brushed his sweet baby face right next to mine. Not saying a word, he walked out of the room. Gosh, his face was so smooth. Flustered, I buried my head back in my exam paper, embarrassed by the display of familiarity but also worried that my brain had left me in the instant that I was about to crack the hardest question on the paper. I eventually walked out of that exam hall annoyed by the fact that I had lost precious time obsessing over what the heck just happened with Lawrence but also with a delicious feeling of anticipation in my heart knowing that Midowa had either seen or would somehow be hearing of that beautifully manly display.

The next day when I ran into Lawrence, he walked over to whisper in my ear, and the heat of his breath wash over me.

"So you're Midowa's wife, ehn? Hmm, just tell him to hold you tight o. If not, I have plans for you." I huffed at him and walked away, not missing the revelation that Midowa had declared that I was his wife.

Haaa!

Chapter 6

ODDS AND ENDS

hip whip whip.

The sound of hair extensions whipping through the air filled the room as I sat cross-legged on the floor of Aunty Zubaida's apartment. I had finally taken out my braids as Nayana advised, and after one week, I could not wait to get them redone. Thank God Aunty Zubaida was able to braid my hair; otherwise, I would have had to scout around to find the one place that would charge me at least $150. In Nigeria I would use that money for a classy boutique splurge.

Aunty Zubby, I would text her whenever my hair was due for braiding, calling her by a pet name to butter her up. To which she would reply, Ehen, smallie. How far?

Please, when can you help me braid my hair?

Aunty Zubaida would respond sarcastically. Come, smallie. Am I your mother?

I would then promise to do her some favour in return, which Aunty Zubaida would decline and then remind me that she's busy living a fabulous life and would be making the greatest sacrifice of her time to touch my hair. I would then praise her and shower her with words of adulation before being dismissed with this: Bye, smallie.

I wondered when Aunty Zubaida would realize that I was no longer the eight-year-old she acquired as a baby sister years ago. I certainly didn't mind that she looked out for me, fussing over my well-being and constantly checking on me when I was at Pitt. I always joked that Aunty Zubaida would have to list me as her first child when she started to have her own children. If she ever had children.

Aunty Zubaida shared her apartment with three other housemates, two of whom were university international students. It was a three-bedroom flat nicely decorated with classic Ikea minimalist furniture.

Aunty Zubaida took pride in the interior decor of her apartment. She had an eye for aesthetics and wanted to make a career of it. Her sister thought that was not good enough and begged her to do something more lucrative.

"Become somebody first. When you establish your own career, ehen, then you can do your fashion designing," Muhmee had told her.

I was glad that Aunty Zubaida had made moin moin, and it was piping hot in the kitchen. I missed homemade moin moin. Granted, between Muhmee and me, we always tried to make it right and bring back those good memories, but it was never quite the same. Not even Aunty Zubaida, with her cooking skills, could nail it.

Aunty Zubaida told me how her housemate was so tickled that it was called moin moin.

"She asked me why many Nigerian words come in doubles," Aunty Zubaida said. I chuckled as I realized what a good observation that was.

"Moin moin," I whispered, clutching on to the root of a braid that she was whipping with expert speed.

"Tom Tom," Aunty Zubaida offered.

"Quick quick," I blurted out.

"Small small."

"One one!" We burst out laughing. I had used that very expression when I was describing to her how I wanted my hair braided.

Even the word *double* was often accompanied by another *double*. Aunty Zubaida said that she had dismissively answered the housemate, saying we repeat words for emphasis. I had never really thought about it, but now in comparison I agreed that Nigerian speech was rife with unexpected words and expressions. We would say the word *beaucoup* to signify many and ask to have a tête-à-tête with someone. Vestiges of the colonists and the language they had cajoled or coerced the people into assimilating.

Aunty Zubaida caught me up on juicy gist about her housemates. She had apparently established herself as the big sister to all of them, the voice of reason. I could not help but marvel at the fact that my aunt would really try to counsel anyone else. Perhaps it was a healthy cycle: her big sister would scold her, and she would then pay it forward.

The feel of Aunty Zubaida's hand on my head and her looming presence took me back to Nigeria, to the darkness of late nights when she would weave my hair hurriedly for school the next day. I reminisced about the three-bedroom flat we had lived in and the neighbourhood, which was a mixture of the rich, the middle class, and the outright poor. We would gossip about Muhmee all night, cackling like midnight witches in Nollywood movies.

"Aunty Zubaida, when will we go to Nigeria again?" I asked, daydreaming about experiencing Nigeria with my aunt once more. We had all changed since moving to the US and had started to view our home country differently. I did not entirely like the change but learned that it was inevitable.

"You and who? I don't have any business in Nigeria o. Please me, I have big plans here." Aunty Zubaida's voice was thick with superiority.

Apparently, no one in the family seemed too interested in going back to Nigeria. I knew that Aunty Zubaida loved being in the States but that she also missed life in Nigeria. What I really wanted to know was if she thought much of the fact that she had come to be in the US because of Dahdee.

I could still hear Muhmee's shout of jubilation the day we found out we would be leaving Nigeria.

After the hundredth time of Muhmee telling me that she didn't have any updates, she finally got the call from Dadee saying our application was finally approved. Muhmee screamed in a way that jolted me out of my study desk, praying that it was what I had been hoping for. She showered the customary praise on Dahdee, calling him the crown on her head and such. I ran from the parlour to the kitchen, searching Muhmee's face with a wide grin when she screamed out, "We are going to America!" Dahdee was sending the papers by email, and we were to start preparing immediately. I shook Aunty Zubaida in excitement, and she solemnly carried on washing dishes. Muhmee got off the phone and broke into dance and song, shouting praises to God. Aunty Zubaida's mood had shifted, and she very surprisingly did not join her sister in jubilation. I hugged Muhmee and went over to hug Aunty Zubaida, who gave me the cold shoulder. I left them both in the kitchen and danced to my room, daydreaming about the day we would eventually leave.

Muhmee was still in a fabulous mood later that night, gyrating and praising the Lord well into the early morning. She hadn't even taken note of the fact that I was mirroring Aunty Zubaida's sour mood. I could only guess at the reasons for my aunt's unhappiness, and I was concerned that whatever was bothering her would dampen my joy.

I noticed an especially heavy-handedness as Aunty Zubaida braided my hair for school the next day. I also noticed some sighing and thickness in her breath as she worked. I started reciting the things that I was going to do before the trip to America, all the goodbyes and I-told-you-so's I would bestow upon the naysayers who doubted that I would ever get to go. When Aunty Zubaida didn't say anything, I concluded that she was probably sad about leaving her boyfriend and fan club behind, something that she had often expressed would not be worth the trip to America.

"Aunty Zubaida, will you be able to transfer your courses over there?" I had asked in an effort to help her refocus on other important things to be taken care of in preparation.

"Who told you I'm following you to America?" Aunty Zubaida hissed.

"Ah, Aunty Zubaida, will you now stay here because of that Solomon?" I could feel my blood rising and didn't even realize I was taking it personally. How could my aunty turned big sister think of separating from me because of a man?

"What's this one saying?" Aunty Zubaida's finger got stuck in a tuft of my hair, and she struggled to get it free, a deliberate revenge for my outburst.

"Did your mother tell you that she's taking me to America?" She had stopped braiding and twisted my head to the side as she looked down at me. She continued braiding, her hands picking up momentum and her head occasionally shaking from side to side. I had never even questioned if Aunty Zubaida was going to be allowed to come with us to America. Muhmee had made threats on occasion that the time would come when Aunty Zubaida would no longer see her. I had understood this in the context of Nigerian parents threatening that the day you will look for them and not see them is the day you will appreciate them. Now I was not so sure. Could Muhmee actually leave her sister here in Nigeria with her illness? I doubted that would be the case but geared up to quarrel with Muhmee if it were to be so.

"Oya, go and ask Muhmee now," I suggested with certainty that it would put paid to the matter.

"Please just shut up!" she barked at me. Silence followed in the candlelit darkness of the Nigerian nights. With that last retort, I decided to respect myself and indeed shut up.

I lay in bed for the greater part of that night, my eyes wide open and my brain swirling with questions.

What did the process of getting our American papers actually involve? *Wait, Ejiro had gone to America through the same process, nau. Her father had sent for them after some time.* I thought I had heard that children of parents who win the lottery were at an advantage. I wondered about nieces. Did they have the same advantage? As my brain worked out that puzzle, other concerns had come up in my mind. What would America be like? Would I fit in? Would I be able to date a white boy? Would my father let me? On the subject of my father, what would I find out about his life there? My cynical classmate had scoffed and asked if I was sure that my father was not actually a drug dealer in America with another wife and three children. After that I had seen movie and literature references that painted this picture where men left their families in Nigeria and started a whole new life abroad, much to the chagrin of the abandoned family who would later find out.

That night, because I was so stressed out about the possibility that Aunty Zubaida would be left behind, I had a weird dream where we were both caught in a whirlpool. Somehow Aunty Zubaida had whipped around and hoisted me on her back, crawling through the vortex like Spider-Man. It was not far-fetched, as Aunty Zubaida had fought many times to save me, once even from a ferocious dog.

Two days later, it all came to a head. We had a houseguest, Buchi, a family friend who we called cousin. Aunty Zubaida was sitting on the arm of the couch while the so-called cousin, Buchi, kept inching closer to her, leery as always. She was about an arm's length from him, which was much closer than Muhmee would have approved of, laughing and soaking up his gist. The conversation was animated and loud enough for Muhmee and me to hear in the kitchen. All of a sudden, their voices dropped to a whisper. Muhmee seemed to have grown restless, her movements faster and her mouth lengthening in irritation. I knew my mother well, and I could sense that there was going to be some sort of recourse to the fact that

Aunty Zubaida dared to entertain a visitor so flirtatiously while her big sister slaved away in the kitchen.

"Go call Zubaida!" Muhmee ordered, and I dashed out, knowing that this meant trouble. I went to the living room and started off complimenting Buchi's shoes. As he basked in his own vanity, I chimed in, "Aunty Zubaida, Muhmee is calling you."

Aunty Zubaida gave me a quick look midsentence and continued what she was saying. I went back into the kitchen and noticed that Muhmee had put the tomatoes and crayfish in the mortar with the pestle by the side, ready for pounding. I positioned myself to start the grinding without being told. That's how it goes in a Nigerian home; you stay close to the matriarch in the kitchen, and on cue you perform duties that had been initiated. It was a perfectly orchestrated dance learned automatically. So when Muhmee coldly said, "Leave it," I realized that minutes had passed since I called my aunt. Something big was about to happen. I got up and took my place at a safe distance from her, present for any service but far away enough from the wrath that was sure to come.

Muhmee washed her hands and, picking up her sweeping bubu dress, sashayed towards the living room.

"Aunty, well done, ma." Buchi bowed as he welcomed her into their midst.

"My dear, how is your mum?" she drawled without a hint of cynicism in her voice.

I peeked into the living room just in time to see the mighty hand of justice land on my aunt's face.

"Get inside that kitchen now!" Muhmee barked.

Aunty Zubaida, clutching her face in shock, ran off, not towards the kitchen but to her room. As the smell of the okra soup wafted to my nose, the stench of tragedy for what had just happened mixed with it and made my stomach turn. The evening was done for; Aunty Zubaida was not coming out of her room, and Buchi, knowing what every child with good home training would do in that moment, sheepishly made excuses and left.

Before Muhmee returned to the kitchen, I was halfway done pounding the spices. I also insisted on kneading the backbreaking fufu, eager to placate her of any residual wrath that may fall on me.

Later that night, I heard raised voices coming from Muhmee's room and hurriedly tiptoed to eavesdrop.

"You want to disgrace yourself, abi? Is he toasting you?" Aunty Zubaida was getting reemed out, and I hoped that Muhmee would go easy on her. *Na wa o, Aunty Zubaida sha*, I thought. She was authentically a baddie for defying her sister's summons. I courted the idea that someday I too would be as ballsy to ignore my mother. Noticing that my breathing was echoing on the door, I decided to step back before I gave myself away.

Just then I heard Muhmee say, "Will you carry this useless behaviour to America?"

After the longest hour, the two of them emerged from the room looking sober. Aunty Zubaida had streaks of dried tears on her face, and even Muhmee looked like she had been crying.

"I'm going to America!" Aunty Zubaida shrieked as she came over to hug me. All memory of the apocalyptic slap forgotten, we carried on eating dinner and discussing travel plans.

And so, two months later, with bags stuffed to the zipper, Aunty Zubaida, Muhmee, and I arrived late to the airport after sitting in traffic for three hours. My fingers clutched the armrest of my seat on the plane, and my stomach dropped as it lifted off to the land of good things.

"Efrebor, Efrebor you go wound oh." Those words played in my head during takeoff, as if on cue. It suddenly dawned on me that I had spent the entire morning obsessing about whether my bolero on spaghetti straps and hipster trousers looked American enough and did not say a prayer for a safe journey.

I was grateful that things had worked out for us to finally join Dahdee. All of us, including Aunty Zubaida. I missed the days when we would sit in the living room with Dahdee, sharing our collective struggles to adapt while he laughed at our dramatic expressions.

I could not imagine coming to America alone as so many of my friends did, especially Stella. I knew both sides of the coin, where some people were determined to get to and stay in America by all means while others abandoned the dream, deciding that there is no place like home.

Aunty Zubaida finished the braids and went into the kitchen to take down the boiling water from the pot. I watched her carefully pour it into a bowl, unaffected by the steaming splashes of water flying all over the place.

She came back into the room and set the bowl on the floor behind me. Throwing a towel over my shoulder, she collected the braids into a ponytail and deftly dipped it in the boiling hot water.

I tried to take my mind off the steam getting close to my skin and the tension from the braids pulling. I went back in my mind to the process of settling in to life in America.

A few weeks after we moved to the US, I ventured around the neighbourhood kids. Some of them were friendly enough, but I quickly became aware of my differentness. Their skin tone against mine, their accent against mine, their hair whipping in the biased wind such as mine never could. I was not shocked by this, as I had already been rehearsing in my mind what it would be like living amongst white people. I had greatly looked forward to it. The movies I watched growing up taught me not to gravitate to Black Americans or even Africans when I came to America. What would be the point otherwise? I would have stayed in Nigeria if I was looking for people like me. It was like going to the Cheesecake Factory and ordering a sandwich. I felt the same way about living in southern states where it never snowed. How would I then prove I was truly in America without stories of snowfall to tell and accompanying pictures to show?

"Have you spoken to Grandma since?" Aunty Zubaida was still trimming the loose strands of hair and putting the finishing touches on the braids. I thought how Aunty Zubaida seemed to have had a different outlook from the rest of us when we moved. She maintained and even increased her sense of importance and did not let anyone dare to think they could intimidate her. She used to beat up anyone who crossed her until one girl's parents threatened to have her arrested and deported. Muhmee's wrath came down heavily on her, and she never tried it again.

"Ehn, she's fine," she responded casually to the question. Aunty Zubaida did not have a close relationship with her mother. It was no surprise based on their history. What kind of mother would give up her child so easily to someone else's care? I was not close to Grandma Ufi either but that was forgivable. As a child I may have seen her all of three times for very brief periods. When we moved to America, Muhmee would call me over to greet Grandma on the phone, and the woman would launch into the ceremonial greetings and teases about finding a husband. Muhmee, on the other hand, had remained close to her mother; there was a bond there that I could not understand. My grandmother fascinated me; the woman did not seem to want any ties in life. Other than that Alhaji for whom she would have given up the last of her pride. I wondered if I would ever have the opportunity to someday have an adult conversation with her, figure out what drives her.

"Finished. Oya, bye-bye." Aunty Zubaida packed up all the hair supplies and hurried to clean up the mess she hated to leave after braiding hair.

"Thank you, Aunty. Please, I'm ready for my moin moin." I fiercely swayed my hips into the kitchen to dish my food, the new braids swinging from right to left. I could feel Aunty Zubaida's eyes trailing my movements, and I turned dramatically to see her shaking her head.

"Small rat," she muttered under her breath.

Chapter 7

HOW TO BE

I have never known a woman more complicated than my mother. I decided in my early psychology classes that I had found the diagnosis for Mrs. Azeezat Ofunwa. Indeed, the woman was hot and cold, up and down, just like the bipolar disorder.

Back in Nigeria she was well known in the neighbourhood, first as the wife of a radio presenter, then as the wife of a radio presenter who had relocated to America. The woman had airs about her but was also able to blend into any social circle she found herself in. She would not be caught with her feet in *portorportor*, muddy ground. She was likewise a woman who would leave her car at home and hop into a keke rickshaw just to avoid traffic.

When Muhmee spoke, her voice rang clear in the air, distinct from the cacophony in our neighbourhood. Lagosians would always ask why she had a Hausa accent and then she would have to explain that she grew up in the north amongst the Hausas. In conversations, you were sure to hear her clicking her tongue in derision, sucking her teeth, and clapping her hands with that singsong *It's a lie!* that she liked to say.

My mother had earned a reputation with the agberos in the area when I was growing up. The vagabonds were known to harass people, collecting their money in the day and robbing them at night. I feared them, hoping never to be found in close proximity to them, and shuddered to think what they could do to a small fry like me. When we moved to Lagos, Muhmee had been equally perturbed by their presence. We would run into the lot of them as she took me to school in the morning and on our way back. They mostly harassed the bus drivers and any pedestrians who had the misfortune to be a target, but Muhmee would avoid making eye contact with them and try to drive away as fast as possible.

Until one day as we drove through the street, when I heard them call out in our direction, "Area mama." Muhmee had thrown her hand in an absent-minded wave and given a slight nod. My eyes nearly popped seeing the smirk on my mother's face, her demeanour all of a sudden not the tenseness it used to be.

"Ahnahn, Muhmee. You people are now friends?" I asked, equally amused and embarrassed.

"My dear, don't mind those crazy people. I don't have their time," she bragged.

I pressed to know when the change happened but got nothing.

Aunty Zubaida had the answer. It all started one night when Muhmee needed to make one of her late-night runs to the airport to pick up the shipment of clothes and bags that Dahdee had sent for her to sell. Aunty Zubaida was with her that night, and on their way back, the agberos jumped in the path of their car and ordered Muhmee to surrender her jewellery and money. Apparently, she had calmly removed her gold necklace and bangles and handed them over while assuring the men that they didn't need to do anything rash. Aunty Zubaida said that while she was nervous, her sister's confidence had kept her calm. When the hoodlums asked for her wedding ring, Muhmee had refused and told them the high value of the jewellery she had already given them. She was not giving up her wedding ring, that precious connection to her husband whom she had not seen in years. When the men made to grab it from her, she jumped out of the car with her eyes burning insanely and started shouting at them in a gruff voice, slapping her chest and asking them to approach her only if they had a death wish. As Aunty Zubaida telling the story, she was jumping all over the room, demonstrating how her sister transformed into a lunatic that scared even her. Seeing this display, the men switched their tactic and instead started hailing her, "Mama, calm down now!" and promising to leave her ring alone. Muhmee jumped back in the car and screeched off with a warning to them: "You boys should not try me o if you no won see crase!"

So, for the longest time after that, she was greeted with cheers as their area mama. She never lost her air of importance to any harassment.

It was that air of importance that had won her Dahdee's affection the day they met. Sometime in the early 1990s, Dahdee was at a friend's going-away party in Lagos Island when he spotted a pretty young thing sashaying through the club lights across the room, dressed from head to toe in white. He had thought perhaps it was the host's girlfriend going around to see that everyone was okay when he found out that she was only a guest, one whom nobody in attendance seemed to know. He pursued her while she looked him up and down and, in good old-fashioned colour, dusted her hands half laughing and sucking her teeth in derision. Convinced that this mystery woman had to be someone important, possibly living in one of the island mansions, Dahdee had spent the whole night begging for her address. She had collected his instead, and without any phone numbers to exchange, Dahdee left her that night hoping that she would indeed come find him. He waited three months, and she did not come. He would go around town searching faces in the crowd, hoping to someday run into her. Then one day she showed up at his door, and after much conversation, he found out that after the party she had gone back to Kano where she lived and that she was really just a nobody who had somehow managed to gatecrash the event in fabulous clothes she had borrowed from her friend. It was all so scandalous, and apparently Dahdee was into that sort of thing. Soon they were married, Muhmee with the good fortune to have landed a middle-class Lagos boy and Dahdee with the shame of marrying a stranger from a questionable background.

This was the woman my mother was, but that seemed to change in the US. I watched her with friends who didn't know her background and saw her attempts to impress them. One such friend in particular was to me an unfortunate reminder of the person Muhmee used to be.

"My sister see me o." The visitor dusted her hands in characteristic surrender.

Mrs. Dopesi and Muhmee sat perched on the couch catching up on the latter's recent visit to Nigeria.

She narrated to Muhmee her cousin's dubious corporate climb and how typical it was in the banking sector.

"Well, I'm happy for her sha. At the end of the day, she made something of herself and is helping the family too." Muhmee shook her head and commented on how her own sister, Zubaida, is prone to such mischief.

I walked in from work starving and hurriedly greeted the women.

Aunty Silvia asked me about work and everything else. I responded in my sweetest voice and left them to get changed and eat dinner. With a mound of rice and stew heaped on my plate, I started to go to my room when the woman called my name.

"Ehen, see what I even said I will tell you o, Samira."

"Yes, Aunty?" I walked into the living room and sat down beside Muhmee as the woman continued. It is not Nigerian custom to sit in their midst while your parents entertained guests, unless you were invited to.

"My cousin who works in Serendipity Bank was telling me of one program they are running this year. It's something about awetism. They are bringing some professionals from America to come and educate people about it."

I shifted in my seat and pulled closer.

Networking with professionals, I thought, chewing my food rapidly.

"Really?" I looked from Muhmee to the visitor.

"My dear, I was just thinking of you when she said it. This type of thing will be good if you can get their contact information and work with them. All you psychology people." She leaned in and slapped my arm meaningfully. As a Nigerian child, I had defied the convention of being the medical doctor or lawyer or engineer. I had overheard too many patronizing conversations when a relative or family friend asked my mother what I was studying.

"My dear, she said it's psychology that she wants to study o!" Muhmee would explain as if to pacify the shamefulness of my career choice.

"Ehn, ehn, and what does she want to do with that?" the other party would ask in disbelief.

"Ah, my dear, she will work with mad people now. There are many of them here," Muhmee would conclude and then digress with a question about some juicy detail of the other person's life.

I was always left feeling the same way, like they were all silently chastising me for such a foolish endeavour on my part.

Who goes to four years of school to study psychology? Why such a wasted effort? Why not just bend your head down and study medicine?

And that's what it all came down to: The smart ones studied medicine, law, and engineering and then the rest who are bleating idiots or perhaps suffering a case of low ambition went on to study psychology and whatever else. Your career choice gave evidence to the capacity of the grey matter in your skull. The most annoying thing was not the fact that these people offered their unsolicited advice on what I should do for work but the fact that my mother entertained their sympathy with the same resignation as did the father of the prodigal son. Dahdee, on the other hand, was more reassuring, perhaps because he too had faced career disappointment.

"Hmm, Aunty, that's interesting o." I got up and went into the kitchen.

I poured myself a cup of water, and as I drank, I decided that I needed to narrate a particularly interesting observation from work that day.

I heard that the women were still in conversation and waited for a good opportunity to sneak in. Of course, I could just walk into the living room and take a seat with them but that would be rude, unbecoming of a Nigerian child with home training.

"Hmm, na wa for this country o!" I kept my eyes on Aunty Silvia as her head bobbed in that characteristic way of Nigerian women, with an eye squint to show that what they are saying is solid gold that they have decided to let their friend in on.

This was the renowned Mrs. Dopesi, a woman so pompous I could not understand what sustained my mother's friendship with her. I knew that it was people like her who had shamed Muhmee into enrolling in nursing school. She thrived on telling other people how to live their lives, like she had it all figured out. Then again, I needed a contact of some sort to follow up on this information I had just heard.

I would ask Muhmee later to get it from her. I was done with the woman's shenanigans at this point. I gobbled down the rest of my hot rice in the kitchen and made my way up the stairs when my phone buzzed in my pocket. It was a message from Nayana: Jaron and I broke up.

I liked to think that I had convinced Nayana to go to Nigeria, but she claimed it was a necessary getaway after breaking up with her boyfriend. Her cousin was getting married and had promised to give her the time of her life and possibly find her a new man. After seeing pictures of her cousin's fiancé and his friends, Nayana had decided that maybe some fine Nigerian guy would change her perspective. That, and she had a photography competition to enter, so she was going to take as many pictures and videos as possible from the motherland.

"Hmm, I find it funny that you would enter pictures from Nigeria when you never wanted anything to do with the place," I started, watching her pack her Nikon camera in a suitcase. It had been a month since the breakup with Jaron, and I knew Nayana was especially hurt that he had been cheating on her. I was proud of her for getting rid of the loser and better still finally going home to Nigeria. But I was annoyed by the hypocrisy that she was only using this trip as a revenge game for when she returns, renewed from finding herself in the mountains of Africa and becoming more than Jaron would ever deserve.

"Yeah, what's wrong with that? I might as well take what they have to offer over there," Nayana responded. "I'm really not looking forward to hearing that annoying accent, but who knows? There might be a really cute guy there for me."

I shook my head, lying on my side with my left hand supporting my cheek.

"It's all good. Midowa will introduce you to some of his friends. There's one I really think you'll like."

"Cool, cool."

"Wait—so when is your ticket for again?" I asked.

"The eighteenth. I think we leave for DC at two p.m. and then take off for Lagos at five," Nayana responded, putting outfits together to see what matched. The trip was still a month away, but it seemed she needed to be doing something to occupy her mind.

"Hmm, I've heard of those direct flights. I don't think I can do it. That's too long to be in one plane."

"Right, I hate layovers. If I could get a flight directly from here, it would be great to just get it over with."

"Yeah. Too bad Mabo and Tobi can't go with you."

"Tuh, please! Those boys have no desire to go to Nigeria. My parents would have to drag them in chains."

"Chai, that's too bad. They don't know how much fun they would have there." It was not lost on me the fact that for ones like Nayana and her brothers, it would be hard to have a positive view of their heritage when they hear only bad stories.

"I'll send you Midowa's number. You can connect with him when you settle down. He'll show you some cool places."

"I'm sure my cousins can take me," Nayana responded, looking at the few items she had in the suitcase. She sank into the bed with a huge sigh. She had thrown in a pair of skimpy-looking shorts, and my eyes were still fixed on them.

"Sharap, I'm sure they won't know Lagos as well as Midowa. Besides, you need to meet your future brother-in-law." I winked at her.

"Uh …" Nayana started and then trailed, off running her hand through her relaxed hair.

She was cooking a smart-ass response as she always did, perhaps some comment about how she couldn't believe I had not dated any other guy since moving to the States.

I did have my share of crushes, though.

The biggest one being my half-French green-eyed nemesis, Jean Luc, in sociology class. He had the most fantastic face I had ever seen on a person. His keen gaze during my class presentations sent painful chills through my entire body. He would stop me in the hallway and ask questions about where I was from and what my life was like. He was interested in me. Genuinely, it seemed. His eyes sparkled when I talked, and seeing that, everything about my life seemed all of a sudden, to my own hearing, wonderful. One day after a presentation, he asked about my experiences in the US, and without thinking, I blurted out, "How about I tell you over a cup of coffee?"

Imagine me, Samira Ofunwa, drinking coffee. Since when?

I couldn't believe he accepted my invitation. But what I couldn't believe even more was that I had the nerve to ask a guy out, just like I had seen on American TV. By the time I caught up with my senses, it was an official date. I had told Aunty Zubaida all about it, and she dished her share of outrageous recommendations on how to dress and conduct myself.

Nothing had ever happened with Jean Luc, not that I truly wanted anything to. I was just happy to tell everyone about the gorgeous white boy who had a massive crush on me. It didn't seem to matter because soon enough I noticed that Jean Luc was always with a model-looking girl from another class. Typical with university guys—they viewed girls as interchangeable.

Not Midowa. He always told me I was different.

Different.

Whether it was in a good way or a bad way, he never elaborated. All I knew was that was the reason he claimed I would always be the one for him.

"Tuh!" I was roused by Nayana's scoffing as she pushed her suit-case to a corner. I knew it had something to do with my relationship with Midowa.

What does the foolish girl know?

For her it was simple: There was only one country she called home. She had no idea that my existence paralleled two worlds, two realities. I couldn't just choose things that would keep me in the US when I have a family—a whole identity—still in Nigeria. There was a weight that rested on me, placed by friends, family, and posterity, that I had to succeed for their sake as well as mine. I had acquired a new status by moving to the US and that status superseded any romance.

That new status, however, did not come without consequences. When the neighbour's kids crinkled their noses while throwing fleeting glances at me, fresh off the proverbial boat, I saw how my new world was as distant to me as it had been on TV. Perhaps even more so, as it became clear that I would never fully fit in no matter how long I lived here. After a couple of incidents, I became very self-conscious about my smell, a thing that I had never experienced before.

"Ugh, it's Muhmee's food that is always smelling all over the house, and it will now stay on my clothes!"

I would complain to Aunty Zubaida when she was still in the house with us. In desperation, I would tie my next-day clothes in a plastic bag and hide it in the back of the wardrobe to shield them from the smell of my mother's soup spices. Over time, this seemed to help, until I realized my clothes smelled funny also because of the mothballs in the suitcase they had been stored in.

In the end it seemed like the restless dream of coming to America and living happily ever after was a fantasy. I slowly began to understand the machine that operated around me—the system that had been designed to shape my identity and aspirations in the so-called land of the free. No wonder the professor always argued that I cannot separate myself from the plight of my African American colleagues. Still, I made a conscious effort not to think about it, to carry on and make the most of myself and remember my true identify—that of where I come from. As Aunty Zubaida would always say in pidgin, "Please, we come from far." But in reality, the US was now home to me, a place where I had invested so much energy to belong. I had learned to imitate the oyibo accent and to use words like *copacetic*, my tongue hanging thickly to my palate on the *t*.

But sometimes I wondered if my life would have been easier if I had resisted any effort to assimilate, leaving my heart whole for my home country, Nigeria.

The next day on my work break, I read up on the welfare grant from Serendipity Bank and the programs that they had been designated to. Muhmee had not yet obtained the number from Aunty Silvia, and I got tired of waiting. Under the autism awareness outreach program, I found a phone number and dialled it. It was answered after a long ring.

"Yes, who is calling, please?" said a woman on the other line whom I suspected was not as old as she was making out to be. Her voice held no enthusiasm for conversation, no matter the answer I had given.

"Good day, ma. My name is Samira. I would like to find out some details about a program at your bank. I won't take your time, ma," I added, acknowledging that although it was still morning for me, it was near closing time for banks in Lagos.

"Please, which program are you talking of?" I had forgotten how Nigerians can turn the word *please* into an assault. I went on to explain that I had heard about an awareness program for autism and wanted to know the details.

"Please, you need to talk to my oga. Please, where are you calling from?" The sneer in her voice was palpable.

I hesitated. "I'm calling from the US. I was hoping to get information on how to volunteer. I—"

"You are not the only one. We have many people from abroad that want to volunteer."

I did not know this woman, but it was evident how she felt about people coming from the States to participate in community programs. I didn't blame her. In the history of Africa, there have always been foreigners wanting to come and save the people from themselves.

"Our manager's name is Mr. Benson Okorocha. Let me give you his number. Hold on." I imagined the scowl on the woman's face as she searched for the phone number, a scowl that would be reserved for anyone other than a customer she could benefit from.

"Thank you very much, ma." I could not believe how ingratiating I was being with this rude woman who may not even be that much older than me. But that's just what you do when you want something from such people—you stoop to conquer.

"Is he in the office right now?" I asked.

"I don't know. You can try your luck." Indeed, it would very well take luck to actually speak to the manager and get anything useful out of him. I dialled the number she gave me, and it rang endlessly. There was no such thing as leaving a voice mail, so as the woman said, I would have to keep trying my luck.

I guess it's back to Aunty Silvia. I sucked my teeth and entered the building to find Dorcy.

⸺⸺⸺

"How is that your boy at work?" Midowa asked later that evening, and I heard the tiredness in his voice. I had caught him at night-time in bed, worn from the day but still pushing through for my sake. He would spend the whole time talking to me until sleep finally took over. I often prompted him early to go to bed, but he would resist until he had only about three hours left to get ready for work.

"He's good o. Today he was playing with my earrings, so we're connecting. Hey, have you heard about a program that Serendipity Bank is doing for autism?"

"You mean here in Lagos? No o. I haven't heard anything like that. All these banks, what's their business with autism?"

"Please, can you help me ask people and see if anybody knows anything?"

"No wahala." He sighed. "Meanwhile, there's one boy on our street who I think may have that autism."

I shifted in my bed. "Why do you think so?"

I was sure that this was the classic medical student syndrome that I had in school days, assigning diagnoses to everyone I knew. But then again, I wanted to hear his logic.

"The boy is just weird. He's always with his mother, and there's something about the way he walks and shakes his head."

"Hmm. Do you know the family well?"

"No o. I always greet the woman sha. She always looks tired, and that's another thing that makes me think something is wrong with the boy. I see her husband too sometimes, but the man always looks angry."

I laughed. "I miss how nosy we can be in Naija. Ahnahn, now you already know the family's history."

"Ah, this one is that they even just moved here recently. If not, by now I would have been able to tell you everything."

"Oya, now do some investigating and lemme know how far. Meanwhile, hmm, guess what? Nayana is coming to Naija o. She just told me yesterday."

"Are you serious? Hmm. I wonder what's pushing her."

"She's finally waking up to reality, when Black Americans sef are randomly moving to Africa, an African will now refuse to come and know her roots. God has opened her eyes."

"Hehe. I miss you, smallie," he said after a brief pause, his voice now a little more than a whisper. "When are you coming home, nau? I don't even know what I will do when I see you."

My breath hung as I imagined that the next time we see each other, he would cup my narrow chin in his hand and examine my face, gulping in every detail like it was the most incredible thing he had ever seen. Just like he used to do when we were in school.

"I don't even know, mehn. I can't wait, honestly. I need to come and eat good food and, ugh, I miss my mango," I answered, returning to the conversation.

"Ah, and now is mango season sef. You need to see the one I ate the other day, kai!"

I imagined the golden yellow and red mangoes tumbling out from a basket, an amazing scent of deliciousness wafting in the air.

"Ah, I'll try to come during the season then. It's been too long since I had a good mango."

"Okay. Remember, it's like April to August, so if you're coming for the next one, that's like the next nine months or so." I heard a question in there.

"Hmm. Let's see sha," I said, catching myself about to make a promise I wasn't sure I could keep. It felt like forever since I left Nigeria, and so far there was no compelling reason to go.

"Wow." His breathing seemed to deepen.

"What?"

"Just the thought of you coming home . . . it's comforting."

"Yeah. I was discussing it with Aunty Zubaida, and it seems like no one else is thinking of going home for now."

"Ehen, I just remembered what I've been wanting to ask you sef. You're AA, right?" His voice came alive as he asked about my genotype.

"Yeah, why?"

"Are you sure?"

"Hian, that's what is on my hospital certificate, nau."

"Hmm. Try and see if you can check again there. I've been hearing of people that have been rechecked, and it was actually something else. I suggest you have them do it there."

Midowa's genotype was AS, and he had asked what mine was as soon as he found out my aunt was a sickler. I remember how deeply he sighed in relief and how devastated he would be if it turned out to be something different. Being raised in Nigeria, we both knew too well what a tragic mistake it was for two people with the sickle cell trait to get together. My aunt was the product of such a mistake, and even though Midowa had never said it, I knew he condemned my grandparents for it.

"Do people in America talk about that, as in the whole genotype thing?" Midowa continued.

I scoffed. "I've never heard it in any context."

I thought about Aunty Zubaida and what the future would be like for her. If she lived long enough to get married and have a child, she would have to make sure her mate had the right genotype. I hoped that the full extent of her recklessness would not go far enough as to risk having a sickler child. Every born Nigerian knows that any romance between a couple where both had the S trait was taboo and doomed to a sure end before marriage.

Boy meets girl.

Boy believes he has found solid wife material—someone who will make a fantastic mother to his children.

Girl informs her family that she has found the man of her dreams.

Boy and girl find out that they both have the AS antigen.

End of relationship.

Genotype compatibility was high on the matching list for a Nigerian.

There was no other choice. Those two Ss would likely mix and produce a child with sickle cell anaemia. Who would deliberately plan for such a fate? For constant hospitalization, a painful existence, and possibly early death? Until medicine caught up with a way to manage the disease, it remained the bane of a number of existences. I could not imagine, with my untainted AA blood, how my entire life trajectory could have been changed otherwise. Midowa and I would never have made it past that initial conversation.

"Sweetheart, please go and sleep. It's late." I started to feel a sense of panic at the thought that my genotype might be wrong.

"Okay, babe. Please greet your parents for me. Good night." Midowa ended the call, and I decided to look into getting retyped.

Chapter 8

GREEN-EYED MONSTER

I knew I liked the boy Midowa in the adjacent SS2 class. We always found a way to speak to each other during recess and used our friends to exchange messages. It was only a matter of time before Midowa would profess his love for me, and every occasion seemed like it would be it. He was already telling people that I was his wife.

It was excursion day on a weekend for the whole set of SS2 classes, and we had gone to Whispering Palms Beach in Benin republic. It was not my particular thing because I found the beach scary and believed that the water was cursed from all the spiritual sacrifices that church members performed there. But I was excited to go because Midowa would be there. It was an uneventful outing save for the music on the beach that gave kids an excuse to get close. I managed to find the right moment to sneak near to where he was with his friend. We made small talk. He was a good swimmer, and I was not. A tour guide had appeared to show us some artefacts, and the crowd of students had somehow shaken Midowa far from me. At first I searched for him discreetly but then started to stretch my toes and neck over the sea of student heads. I suddenly spotted him with his eyes looking in my direction, as if he too had been looking for me.

My heart skipped, and I adjusted my knapsack from America and turned my face forward to peer at the guide as if suddenly realizing he had something to say. We were dressed in school uniforms but were permitted to change into mufti after the tour. For the rest of the day, it seemed that Midowa was always far from me talking to someone yet throwing adoring looks my way. I wished he would come talk to me but then again I didn't. What would I say? Would I be cool or awkward? It was agonizing to think that he was right there in the same space as me, watching and aware of me but still maintaining distance. I checked my internal mirror to make sure I looked my best. I hoped I was cool enough in my senior girl pencil skirt and shirt neatly tucked in with a neck tie. I was no more that gangly junior girl wearing a pinafore that would swallow up my figure. No, I was now in the appearance of a woman to be taken seriously and desired. That meant I had to constantly obsess about my looks, especially now that someone's attention was fixed on me.

I loved and hated it at the same time.

Finally, we made it back to school after sitting in traffic. I was annoyed because Midowa ended up on another bus from me. I would have been content staring at the back of his head during the ride. One thing, though, had comforted me throughout the trip. I looked down at my hand at the empty wrapper of the delicious burger I had enjoyed, courtesy of Midowa. When we had piled up in the bus to leave, someone sitting in front handed me the beach-made burger, saying that Midowa had sent it. I smiled and collected the food very gingerly, not ashamed to act coy as assumption hung thick in the air. Yes, student spectators would know that I was indeed his wife.

As we got off the bus, I hoped—no, I prayed—that he would be hanging around for me. I dusted my hands on my hipster trousers as I walked towards the steps of the bus, adjusting my bra strap to make sure it was safely tucked into my yellow peasant blouse. I had to see Midowa before I went to sleep that night. I had a feeling—a sweet feeling that even sweeter things would be said between us and that those things would fill my dreams for the one night I would be spending in the school dormitory.

I got off the bus and coughed as the fumes from the decrepit vehicle poured into my nose. I stood there for a minute and coughed discreetly while looking over at the bus across the street to see when Midowa would get off. I looked up and saw him jostling his friend as he jumped off the bus. My legs turned to jelly, and I willed them back to life.

As he approached me in the darkening night, he pushed his glasses up his nose and fixed his gaze on me. I didn't know whether to inch closer to him or just stand there looking unbothered. Before I could decide what to do with myself, I felt his hand clasp tightly around mine. We walked a few steps, and I almost bumped into him when he stopped abruptly. I collected myself from the tingling electricity that shot through my body as I absorbed the intimacy of the moment. A car sped past, and I realized that we were about to cross the street and could have walked right into the vehicle. Midowa squeezed my hand tighter, signalling that it was safe to proceed, and I followed him, sheepish and light-footed like I was floating on a cloud. We crossed the street over to the front gate of the school that was now teeming with kids excitedly chatting and screaming, prolonging the day's extracurricular activity.

"Boys, e go be tomorrow now!" Midowa called good night to his buddies, suddenly pulling his hand free from mine while his other hand clutched his backpack. The boys oohed and aahed suggestively at the two of us as Midowa smiled and shook his head. Except for the occasional word about random things that happened at the beach, we walked together silently towards the girls' dormitory. As we reached the front of the hostel, Midowa rubbed the back of his head as it hung slightly low. Something had happened in that short stroll from the school gate to the hostel. Midowa was increasingly chuckling unnecessarily, and my annoyance had grown with every step. I was irritated not because I detected nerves in the tone of his laugh but because he had dropped my hand so fast in front of his guys like it was contraband. How quickly he had let go and ruined a perfectly dreamy moment. Why did he take my hand in the first place? Did he think I couldn't cross the street by myself and needed to be led like a child? Was he just playing big brother to me like he did to everyone else? Or maybe he was ashamed to be seen with me. Maybe . . .

Those questions were swimming in my head when he touched my hand and I faced him.

"Sorry. I hope my friends didn't embarrass you," he said as his eyebrows furrowed.

I shrugged and glanced down briefly before looking back at him. "Thank you for the burger," I said without much gratitude.

He nodded and continued to gaze at me. I stared up at him, and my pout dissolved as I realized he was about to say or do something.

"I'll see you tomorrow," he whispered, rubbing the back of his head.

I shut my mouth, which was hanging open in anticipation of some wonderful expression and managed to wish him a good night. I turned around and walked towards the dorm room where class-mates would surely be twittering about their escapades that day at the beach.

"Sweet dreams," Midowa called to me in a distant hoarse voice that I could not interpret.

Sweet dreams indeed.

Those were fun times. It was all so dramatic and intoxicating the idea that Midowa would claim me and we would share an uncomplicated future together. Now the thought of commitment weighed on me like a bag of cement. There were many things at stake, decisions to be made. None of which I was in the mood for.

Muhmee had just returned from work, and I caught her heading up the stairs.

"Muhmee, welcome," I greeted her and took her handbag.

"Ehen, shey there's food?" she asked.

"Yes, Mum. I made Jollof rice and turkey," I replied, setting her bag down on her vanity.

"Good. Please, I don't have energy to cook today."

"Muhmee, have you heard from Aunty Silvia about the program?" I asked.

"No o. Take her number and ask her, abeg." She must have had a rough day with patients, judging by the raw irritability in her voice.

"Mummy! Mummy!" I tapped her back with a wicked smile as she handed me her phone.

"My friend, leave me alone, jor. Nobody should disturb me this morning. I need to sleep."

"Thanks, Mum." I got the number and went back into my room. I plopped on the bed planning for a lazy Saturday of Nigerian movies. I tossed my phone aside, prepared to put off the call as long as possible. I did not like that woman at all and knew I would have to grovel because Mrs. Dopesi did not give anything without making you beg.

"Ughhh." I groaned and picked up my phone as I heard Aunty Zubaida's voice chastising me for being spoiled and letting my parents do everything for me.

I dialled the number. If only I was more like Aunty Zubaida, by now I would have Mrs. Dopesi doing my bidding.

"Hello?" The woman's voice cut through my thoughts, and I instantly took offense at that annoying inflection she always put on. You just knew from hearing her accent that it was manufactured to oppress the folks back home who were not as fortunate to be in America. It was because of people like her that some would give anything to have the opportunity to come to America so that they too can wear that phonetic badge of honour.

"Hello, Aunty." My voice dropped a few decibels to convey my subservience. "It's Samira."

"Ehen, Samira. How are you, dear?" she replied, her words dragging like speech was a gift to be bestowed in small doses.

"I'm fine, Aunty. How's the family?" I twittered.

Once I had fulfilled the customary pleasantries, I asked about the autism program, and Mrs. Dopesi insisted that she wished there was a way she could take me to Lagos herself. How typical. Nigerians will not only give you directions to do something but also must show you. Whether it is really out of concern that you can't do it yourself or just to establish that they have done you a favour to be repaid, it was quite condescending.

"When are you people planning to go to Nigeria sef? Me, I'm going beginning of next year. You know me. Because of my business, I'm always back and forth." Aunty Silvia laughed in that condescending way she did when she wanted to toot her own horn. "Anyway, even if your parents are not planning to travel, you need to go and see things for yourself. You're now a big girl o!" she continued.

"Yes, ma. Eem, I'm not sure if I can go, but when is the program scheduled for?" I decided not to react to the insinuations and tried to get as much information as I could out of her.

"I think it's this November o, but let me give you my cousin's number in Nigeria. She can tell you better."

With yet another number to call, I decided I had gotten all I could from the woman and bid her a hurried goodbye.

—⁓⁓—

The day finally arrived for Nayana to head to Nigeria. I rode with her in a taxi to the airport. As she checked all her luggage, I couldn't believe her parents had not come to see her off because she has travelled alone before. My parents would have been right there doting and going over minute details with me. There was a certain level of independence that children raised in America are allowed by their parents that would forever be foreign to me. In any case, I was happy to escort my friend to the airport, especially considering where she was going. I had to. Nayana was going to take my place in Nigeria. See the country for me. See certain ones who were dear to me. See Midowa.

I hugged her at the departure point and ran my hands down her arms, making a sad face. I caught myself getting emotional when I said, "I'm so excited for you. You're going home!" She then threw me a questioning look as if to remind me that she was coming back.

I pulled out an envelope from my bag and handed it to her, feeling my eyes well up. I sniffed and looked at her face for an awkward minute.

"Please give that to Midowa when you see him, okay? Shey you have the number? I've told him you will contact him, and you guys can meet up. Oya, come and be going. Have a safe flight. Hey, please text me when you get on the plane, when you take off, and as soon as you're connected in Naija, all right?"

"Yes, Mum," Nayana snickered. "See you when I get back." She turned and walked into security.

Hey, you settled in? I texted her, feeling lonely on the long drive home.

Yup. Gosh, this one guy kept trying to talk to me. You just know he's Nigerian lol, Nayana responded, adding a disgusted face.

Lol. Hmm. You better start practicing your smoothest letdowns cos you're gonna be busy in Nigeria, you know, as a fine girl. I added a wink.

Nayana sent back a smirk.

Bring me back hugs from Midowa.

Uh . . . okay?

Be safe. I added hugs.

When I got home, I felt like the only person left in the world and wished Aunty Zubaida still lived in the house with us. I was going to miss talks with my annoying friend, but more than that I missed Midowa. I missed being in Nigeria and missed all the things that I didn't even realize yet that I missed. I couldn't wait for Midowa to get the letter I had written him. It was a last-minute thought that occurred to me—that even though we communicated by phone, it was a charming reminder that at some point in our relationship that was all we had.

When we first moved to the States, it took months before Midowa got my first letter and then some more months before I got his. The first thing he wanted to know was whether I had tried a banana split sundae and what did it taste like. In reality I was not just prancing around tasting ice cream, but I made sure to paint a wonderful picture of all the incredible things I was getting to do in America.

Those letters meant a lot to me, the three that managed to reach me. I kept them, and even though I didn't know exactly where, it was a comfort that they were somewhere in my possession.

I finally did try a banana split sundae and wrote Midowa to tell him all about it. I had written a bunch of incoherent things in that letter, the most important of which was the fact that I missed him and wished he could just appear for a day. I told him how we would have explored the cathedral together, finding cosy spots to share his Discman. It was two months later that he would get that letter. He wrote back and went through endless strife trying to send it. His parents had apparently advised that it may never reach me, so he was better off going to the cybercafe to make international calls or send an email. So he sent the first email telling me how he wrote a reply but was afraid that it would end up in the Atlantic Ocean. I was happy to hear from him but slightly disappointed that I would not get to see the beautiful slant of his handwriting, so personal that it could not be replaced by any email. We agreed to try a few more times with the letters and eventually gave it a rest.

As digital advancement reached Midowa in Nigeria, it became easier to private chat and talk on the phone. But I still preferred the anticipation of a letter in hand, the feel of someone's bare soul.

I lay in bed late that night, staring at the ceiling. I did not want to turn on my star lamp or talk to Midowa or do much of anything else. I just wanted to think.

Think about the decisions I needed to make. What would I do with my career? What would I do with Midowa? What would become of Aunty Zubaida? Why was I so afraid to make any decision and stick to it? Why did it feel like the happiness I imagined I would find in America no longer seemed to be enough? Would it be better to be all American or all African or both? For an immigrant who comes from a place where tradition is the ultimate thing, sticking to the path well known as tested and trusted by generations past, is it betrayal to reject some of those long-held beliefs and form new ones? Can the past beliefs coexist with new ones?

It gnawed at me how easily Nayana had made the hard decision to go to Nigeria and stick to it. She certainly knew what she wanted to do with the rest of her life. As frivolous as it seemed to me, the girl was following her dream of photography. At this rate she might just fall in love with someone in Nigeria and decide to live there. Even Aunty Zubaida, whom I spent time worrying about, seemed to know what she wanted out of life, however long or short it may turn out to be.

I decided to visit my friend Stella in New York. We always had the best talks, and although Stella didn't agree with some of my new Western ideas, she would at least raise sound arguments.

I need to call Aunty Silvia's cousin in Nigeria tomorrow, I thought as sleep overpowered me.

On the bus ride to work the following Monday, I looked at the number from Aunty Silvia and debated if it was a good time to call.

When I got off the bus, I dialled the number, hoping to have a productive conversation during the fifteen-minute walk from the bus stop to the building.

A woman answered.

"Hello, ma. Please, is this Aunty Tolani Bademosi?" I asked.

"Yes. Who is this?" the woman answered.

"My name is Samira Ofunwa. I got your number from Aunty Silvia. She's a family friend."

"Oh, you're the girl from Pennsylvania, right? She told me you would be calling." I was then greeted with a vibrant hello, which put me at ease. How special it was to call home from abroad; it just made whatever you had to say much more important.

"Yes, ma. She told me that your bank is organizing a program for autism awareness in Lagos, so I wanted to get more information about it."

"Oh yes. She said that you read psychology and just graduated. Congratulations."

"Thanks, Aunty." Of course Aunty Silvia would unload all my business to her cousin, the same way she unloaded her cousin's business to Muhmee.

"Yes, I'm about to go into a meeting now. Call me back this weekend, then we can talk."

I knew how easily this could turn into phone tag, and as much as I had expected to get the runaround, I did not have anymore time for it.

"Okay, Aunty. How about I send you an email with the things I want to know about the program and then you can just take your time and get back to me?" I hoped she would take the bait.

"That works for me. Let me give you my email. It's badetol@ serendipity.org. I'll try to reply as soon as possible."

"Thank you so much, Aunty. I would appreciate that. I really need to get the information to finish a project before the deadline." I felt justified at this point telling a lie.

"Okay, my dear. I'll get back to you. Take care, and greet your mum."

"Thanks, Aunty. Have a good evening." I had reached the grey building and stood outside for a few minutes to finish the call. I knew I was being watched by my colleagues and did not want them to go to the supervisor with a complaint about me being on the phone. The expectation was that once you clocked in with the kids, your phone had to be put away.

I decided I would send the email right away and hope that the woman followed through.

Ms. Rhonda gave me permission to work Monday, Tuesday, and Wednesday so that I could take a weekend trip to see Stella in New York. Stella was the kind of friend who read so richly in stories about the beauty of the human spirit but in real life was a lot to take in. She was an old soul who would tell you off in a minute if you did something wrong and lecture you about all the reasons why it was especially disappointing from someone of your calibre. She scolded so effectively that it was hard sometimes to remember if it was meant as a rebuke or praise when she would remind you of the home training that your parents had lavished on you and of how this current slipup could threaten the very foundation of that training. After this scolding, she would go on to tell you a story that would have you falling to the floor in laughter, forgetting that she had troubled a particular nerve in your soul. By the time you had a chance to process the interaction, you would brush off the offense and conclude that she was just trying to be a good friend.

Stella was the same age as me but anyone would swear she was an older sister, an aunt even.

I woke up early Thursday morning to catch the Greyhound bus headed to New York City. It wasn't as bad as Stella had worried it would be. I kept to myself and tried not to draw attention. Midowa texted to let me know what he had planned. His office was having an in-service day, so he was going to take Nayana out for photographs.

She said you had something for me? Midowa texted.

Yeah, just a small thing. I sent a smiley face.

Hmm. If I had known, I would have gone to meet her since. She just sent me the address. I'm picking up Bankole and then we'll head there.

Okay, cool. I hope she will like him o because she's in Nigeria to find a good man. I sent a wink. I thought it was very prudent that he would be taking his friend. I also thought it strange that it wouldn't have bothered me if he wasn't.

I did wonder if Midowa would find Nayana attractive, with her lean frame and long neck. I imagined that if I asked him, he would say she wasn't nearly as pretty as me and then add that he could never be with a girl who was taller than him.

Midowa and Nayana. I could see how they could be attracted to each other. Midowa would find her arrogant by virtue of her American status. That would turn him off. Then again, he might find it intriguing.

I tried to distract myself from the rogue thoughts circling my brain amidst that bus chatter. I pulled out the *Archie and Veronica Digest* I had picked up from the centre and saved for the trip.

My phone buzzed periodically as Midowa sent me updates. They had arranged to go to the Lekki Conservation Centre first and then to the Nike Centre for Art and Culture. Nayana was only able to take pictures at the conservatory, as it was prohibited in the gallery. Midowa was amused that his friend was changing his accent to an annoying high-pitched drawl. Nayana kept calling the gallery Nai-kee like the shoe brand, but Midowa would correct her and say it's Nee-keh, as in the name Oluwanike.

Babe, you're really missing the drama. Bankole just asked her where she's from. Guess what she said? Midowa texted.

Oh gosh. I can just imagine, I replied.

She said she is originally from Maryland, but she lives in Pennsylvania now.

Yup, that does not surprise me at all

Lol You should have seen the foolish look on his face. He now asked her, no I mean which tribe, and she said, "Oh, my parents are Edo." I pictured his excitement as he watched the drama unfold.

My dear, that's typical. Here in America, kids will tell you that it's their parents who are Nigerian. So foolish.

Na wa o. I've seen many of them like that on the island. It's funny, they are either American or British. Like nobody claims any other identity.

Midowa and I agreed that children abroad born of Nigerian parents had no business claiming any other identity. Apparently, they were not taught that the question *Where are you from?* means where are your parents from, the parents who birthed you and taught you what life is. You may be growing up in a different culture, but does that make you any less Nigerian?

By the time Midowa said he had dropped off Nayana and Bankole, it was close to 11:00 p.m., having spent the greater part of the day wrestling traffic.

The Greyhound bus groaned to a halt at the last stop in New York City, and I hopped on a train to Stella's apartment.

Stella insisted that I text at intervals, saying how much the Greyhound bus crowd worried her. "Abeg o, just mind your business. Don't talk to those people on the bus before they will kidnap you."

"Pray before you go o!" The orders kept coming, and I would respond *Yes, ma* to all of them.

When I finally reached New York and texted Stella, she responded, "Praise the lord! Thank God for journey mercies." Her piety added to her aged persona and was so refreshingly Nigerian. I too had my moments of unequivocal praises and thanks to God for everything.

I'm taking the train now. It's the number 4 shey? I texted my friend. I loved getting around on the train despite of the uneasy feeling of being in the path of some unknown madness that was sure to break out. The busy city truly felt like the capital of the world, with the sticky smell of wear and tear from centuries of too much excitement. New York reminded me of Lagos, and if the two were to team up, New York would be the better-looking pal watching in bewilderment as Lagos showed him how madness truly behaves.

Yes o, number 4. Please don't take 6 even if they say you can change. Just take the 4 and get off at the Binnacle stop. I could almost see Stella rattling off those instructions, her eyebrows raising in firmness as if there was a chance it would be missed.

Hold your bag well o. I no won hear story! I shook my head reading those words, just what I had predicted she would say. This was not my first or second journey to New York, but I was paying for narrating to Stella how I watched a woman's handbag get snatched in the subway on one of my trips.

See you soon. Stella sent a smiley face.

See ya!! In the end we were both excited to meet and gossip into the dead of the night, catching up and synching our lived experiences.

Chapter 9

BRANCHING OUT

The instant I stepped into the apartment building, Stella came flying at me, herself only a head taller. We embraced and chattered the whole way from the elevator to her apartment. She hustled me into the characteristic Brooklyn one-bedroom space as if I was at risk of getting kidnapped. Stella apologized for her modest accommodations, commenting that it was for the have-nots. I shushed her, pointing out how neat and well decorated it was, with wall decals of motivational quotes that reflected her philosophies perfectly. I kept to myself that the pretty flowers and butterflies had almost completely masked the rot of the building.

"What of that your friend Nayana wey no know where she from?" Stella asked me as we lounged in the living room, having showered and eaten fresh eba and okra soup.

Stella was the only person with whom I talked honestly about Nayana. I tolerated her cluelessness about Nigeria and enjoyed filling in the gaps about my beloved country, but there were times when Nayana got on my nerves, and Stella was the one person who would hear all about it. She would then launch into a lament about these oyibo children, meaning Nigerian children born or raised abroad, condemning their lack of culture and even questioning their virtue. I would then have to intervene and defend Nayana's cultural illiteracy and the adorable efforts she makes to educate herself. I soon learned to speak carefully about Nayana for fear that Stella would shred her name to an irredeemable degree.

"She's fine o. She is now officially in Naija. I need to find out how she liked her outing sef. She was touring Lagos today." Stella had already been updated that Nayana had finally decided to go back home, much to her amusement.

"Good for her o. She should go to her village so they can take her to the farm. Let sun hammer her small."

I dismissed the slightly troubling thought that there was a hint of jealousy when Stella condemned Nayana so heavily for things she had no control over. Foremost of which was her status as a born and bred American.

"How is mumsi now?" I quickly changed the subject.

"My dear mumsi is good o." Stella sighed and continued. "Toye is just finishing all her money, ehn. I don't know what is wrong with that boy." She sucked her teeth and continued eating her ice cream with animal crackers.

"Ahnahn, why now? Is he spending her money on his babe?"

"Which babe *hiss*! Please, I even want to know if he has a babe. Maybe the girl can help him get his brain together. Mumsi said he is always talking about business, and she uses her money to help him, but there's nothing coming out of the business. If wishes were horses, I will just package that boy and bring him here so that I can monitor all these shady moves he's making. It's the drugs that are pushing him."

Stella's face bore a faraway preoccupation as she moved around the biscuit crumbs in her lump of dessert.

"Hmm. My dear, by God's grace everything will work out well, ehn. Don't worry. How far with the rehab?"

"Hmm. My dear, I don't even know what they'll be doing there. I'm just imagining how the place will be. We who don't know how to maintain anything good in that country."

"I know, right?" I sighed. "Me sef, I'm thinking of going to Naija o. There's a program they're doing for autism in Lagos. Mumsi's friend connected me to the woman who is organizing it."

"Are you serious? That's good o. At least you have your blue passport now, so you can travel anyhow. Me, I'm going to be stuck here until I get my papers . . ." Stella's voice trailed off as I pictured what it would be like to go back home with my American passport. Nayana arriving in Nigeria with her American accent and American passport. Going through immigration when we first came to the States was an ordeal, and I looked forward to my first opportunity to re-enter as an American citizen. Then it would not feel like I was a criminal coming to do something evil in America, thanks to the blue passport. I was grateful for it but also resented its significance. It created an unfair hierarchy, and I hoped that Stella did not secretly hate me for having the privilege.

"So when do you think you'll be going?" I heard her say.

"The program is in November, but I'm not sure sha. Still thinking about it."

"Okay now. Lemme know what you decide, abeg. If you're going, I'll send you some things to give my mum. It is well o. Abeg, let's watch a movie, nau." Stella pulled out her laptop and set it on the coffee table, moving it closer to us. I got comfortable on the sofa, adjusting the pillows and crossing my legs underneath me. We found a Nollywood movie that looked promising and turned off the lights as we scraped our ice cream to the last.

"My friend, will you come on get away from my front!" A woman on-screen yelled at her son, throwing her shoe at him. We both laughed at the nostalgic exchange, swapping stories of explaining Nigerian expressions to co-workers.

Midowa called me around 9:00 p.m., which was 3:00 a.m. his time.

I excused myself from the movie, self-conscious and hoping that Stella wasn't irritated about the interruption.

"Hey! You're not sleeping yet?" I breathed, trying to be discreet.

"Hey, baby. How far now?" His voice sounded groggy, like he should be sleeping but had stayed up.

"Good. I've settled in and we're watching a movie right now."

"Heya, that's good. Please greet your friend for me. I just finished reading your letter. Thanks, babe. That was so sweet."

"What did you like the most?" I asked.

"The lyrics from the Goo Goo Dolls. They took me back to those days, and my heart almost exploded," Midowa croaked.

I'd included the lyrics to the song "Iris" that we had shared on the night before I came to the States.

The scent of him that night stayed on my brain for a long time, the expensive-smelling cologne that I knew he had snuck from his dad to smell like a man. It was the last night we would see each other before I moved away from home.

Midowa had come to visit as he occasionally did, and Muhmee welcomed him, offering orange juice. Usually, we would chat for a while in the house and then let Muhmee know we were going for a stroll. That night, he had brought his Discman and a present for me. It was a burned CD full of songs that I loved and that would remind me of him.

We sat on the veranda floor, a sweet romantic breeze enveloping us. He played the CD, and we both shared his earphones, my head on his shoulder. Occasionally he pointed to the sky and showed me a twinkling star, just like in the movies. When the song "Iris" came on, my throat suddenly felt tight, and I fought back tears. I squeezed my eyes shut and absorbed the painfully relatable lyrics. As the melody played, I put my delicate fingers in his hand, and he grasped them tightly. I would always scoff when Midowa fanatically argued that the Goo Goo Dolls had made the greatest melody ever with that song, agreeing that it was indeed good. In the fragile moment of that night, listening to the song, I worried that the devastating desire that we felt for each other would not last long enough and that the moment would only remain frozen in our hearts, never to be recreated.

"Sometimes I play that song at night looking up at the sky and wondering if you're doing the same," I said to him.

He chuckled. I could tell he was wiped out but wanted to enjoy the reverie.

"Go to sleep, hon. We'll catch up tomorrow, okay?"

"Okay, love. Please greet Stella for me . . ." His voice trailed off.

"Sure thing. Night." I hurriedly returned to the living room and squeezed back into the comfy couch.

"My dear, sorry o," I apologized to Stella.

"Ahnahn, for what na? Your bobo is more important."

"He said I should greet you." I avoided her eyes.

"Heya, how is he?" Stella asked, scraping her ice-cream bowl.

"He's fine. He was gisting me how he and his friend were harass-ing Nayana for saying she's from Pennsylvania."

"Hmm. Make she no go dey trip for your bobo o." I cringed at the insinuation that Nayana would betray me and regretted saying anything. Stella praised me in the usual manner, pointing out how anyone would be lucky to have me as a friend, especially a lost cause like Nayana. Left to her, I was a friend so pure that the girl didn't deserve me. How many girls would trust their girlfriend around their man, especially in their absence?

"Hmm. That your fine boyfriend so. You think sey if na me I no go collect am from you?" she teased.

We both laughed, but I was not amused.

"Well, my dear, I really pray for you o because you wey no like trouble. Make this girl no come cause trouble for you because na big risk you take so. I no know who go fit send their friend across the seven seas to go visit her boyfriend if no be you."

"No o. I didn't send her to go visit him. I just asked him to assist her with her photography project." I heard the high pitch in my voice, like a child being accused of stealing from the soup pot. I started to feel my stomach tighten, not sure if I was more offended by the idea that my friend would move in on my boyfriend or that I was the idiot who naively orchestrated it.

Stella must have sensed that I was getting defensive and scooped more ice cream into my bowl.

"Abeg, let's see what's happening in this yeye movie sef. Why did they use this girl who cannot act?" She turned the movie back on and adjusted the laptop in my direction.

"My dear, seriously, she's horrible." I shoved a spoonful of ice cream in my mouth and fell back into the ridiculous movie plot that had us doubling over with laughter.

My trips to visit Stella often went like this: We would eat her notoriously delicious Nigerian meals and relax with a cup of ice cream topped with crumbled animal crackers. We would tease each other about our addiction to the dessert and proceed to comb the forest of our lives in diaspora, from Stella's desire to bring her family to America to the disappointments we both came to find now being in the land of our dreams. We would then settle down to a Nigerian movie that was sure to evoke laughter and ridicule with its watery plot and exaggerated acting. We would run commentary on the movie and moan about all the things we missed from our childhood. We would then finish by expressing hopes for the best of both worlds where we could enjoy the comforts of America and still keep a piece of our heart at home.

As we talked into the night, I realized that Stella would have given anything to be in my place, with an opportunity to go back home. I had no excuse not to go. I owed it to her, to our shared consciousness that our gains in America were only as good as our contributions back home. In the end there was nothing that kept me as grounded and thankful as my deep conversations with my dear friend, strong personality notwithstanding.

I headed back to Pittsburgh three days later, deciding that if Aunty Tolani had positive feedback, it would be a sign that I needed to go.

About a week later, I opened my laptop on a Wednesday evening after returning from work to find an email from Tolani Bademosi.

> *Hello, Samira,*
>
> *I'm just following up on our conversation. I think it's a good thing that you are interested in this program. We really need to get the word out there, and young minds like yours would be very useful. So the program is called Hearing the Voices of Autism, and it was started by a group of parents affiliated with our bank that wanted to raise awareness about the diagnosis. Our bank decided to fund the program out of our community welfare grant, and so far we are in the second year of running the program. This year it's scheduled for 4 November, and we have speakers coming from the US. I will send you their names so that you can look them up and see what their areas of interest are. We also get students from the university to volunteer, so let me know if you would be interested in that. If you have any further questions, feel free to reach out again.*
>
> *Best,*
> *Tolani Bademosi*

I read each word meaningfully, picturing the gravity of what they meant. It sounded to me like the organizers were serious about their intentions and vision for the program.

They are having people coming from the US to speak at the event. Wow, how cool.

If people who were not Nigerian felt it was worthy to come to the country to talk about this, then why not a proud Nigerian like myself? I skipped downstairs to tell Muhmee about it but caught her as she was about to leave for work.

"Muhmee, when you come back, I'll show you what Aunty Silvia's cousin sent me," I called out to her as she grabbed her keys. I added goodbye and watched her through the window as she went to her car. It struck me how her body language had changed from the way it was in Lagos. There Muhmee carried herself slowly, deliberately, with a sense that time belonged to her. Now she had an urgency in her step and a sort of uncertainty about her movements.

I wondered if she ever told her co-workers about the crazy things she did back home. Like the day we went to the city market, bustling with too much commerce, chaos, and body contact. The Lagos market was the most intimate crowd to be in, so intimate that a person's wallet could innocently find its way into someone else's hands. I got a fair warning from Muhmee, albeit at fifteen years old, to hold on tightly to her arm in the crowd. My biggest fear was always that someone would grope me. It had happened before, and my mother had raised fury, drawing the support of others who condemned the irresponsible young man and pleaded with her not to fight him.

That day as we made our way through the sweaty sea of people, I held my breath periodically, hoping that we would soon settle in one shop where I would get some personal space. Just as we went to turn a corner from a group of young men who were lurking in front of a stall, I felt a man 's hand slap and grab a handful of my butt. I shivered, the iciness of shame washing over me. I wished the ground to take me, hide me from the awkward confrontation that would require me to acknowledge the violation of my innocence.

"Who touched you?" Muhmee bellowed, realizing what had happened.

Ugh. I didn't want to speak. It would have been better to just keep going and pretend nothing happened.

"Him." I pointed towards a sand-coloured specimen who was grinning and licking his lips.

"Ah, madam. I will marry this your daughter o. Just dash am to me." The guys around us laughed and eyed my curves greedily.

Muhmee sighed, and I tensed, waiting for the disgrace of watching my mother fight a grown man in public. It had happened before, and as much as it would have served the creature just right to get a taste of her madness, I didn't want to see it again.

In a mind-boggling twist, Muhmee instead managed to grab the man's hand, making him follow us around the market carrying our goods, all the while admonishing him in a chillingly calm voice to be more respectful to women.

Muhmee was no longer that person. There was a marked difference in her from the exciting woman she was in Nigeria. Now when she spoke to Americans, her voice took on a strange tone so unnatural that I knew it was taxing to have conversations day in and day out. In public she appeared to be a quiet woman, a far cry from the area mama she was acclaimed to be in Lagos. Now she seemed only like a woman carrying a heavy load.

Was she happy? I could honestly not tell. I believed that she had yearned to come to America, amongst other reasons to be with her husband. They seemed to love each other all right; Dahdee certainly paid good enough attention to his wife. I was convinced that unlike my schoolmate had once suggested, Dahdee did not so much as look at another woman in the years they were separated.

As for Muhmee . . .

No. I wasn't ready to process the thought that was gnawing at me.

At this point, I wondered if Midowa also noticed that the relationship was becoming redundant. I had sent him the letter hoping that it would give us something fresh to talk about. Being apart for so long, we relied on the memories of our time together to keep things interesting. Midowa seemed to have enjoyed the trip down memory lane from our school days.

Later that night, I caught up with him lying in bed. I was tired from the day and thankful that Muhmee had made dinner and served Dahdee. I wanted to tell him that I was almost certain that I would be coming home but wanted to confirm that everything was in place.

Yeah, that poor kid has been so medicated, he even needs medicine to poop. I was often the one talking about my day with the kids at the centre. While I thought it sweet that Midowa was content listening to me, I found the one-sided conversations tedious.

Na wa o, I just wonder how life is for people like that. I can't imagine it, Midowa texted back.

That's what I was discussing with my supervisor, the concept of self-actualization for someone with a severe disability or mental illness or both.

Ehen, please, what exactly is this self-actualization thing you keep talking about sef?

Basically it means reaching your full potential as a person, as per being the best you can be.

As what? I often detected sarcasm in his questions when we discussed subjects like this.

Whatever you want to be. Like you now being a successful architect and living comfortably, your name all over the newspapers and TV. I sent a wink.

Ehn, ehn, so that will now make me a happy person? What of family? Or God? Where do they come in?

Well, yeah, that's part of it. It's about an individual's intrinsic sense of accomplishment. I searched my brain for any reference on spirituality in Maslow's hierarchy and how that would fit in.

Hmm, see Efiko, A+ student. You sound like a textbook, he quipped.

I didn't respond for a while, so he continued.

All I know is that this American idea of self is what is worrying them. When they will not make time for God or family. I've just noticed all the developed countries are the least religious people and with the worst mental health problems. Somebody will wake up and decide to just go kill random strangers in the name of mental health. A little bit of gratitude will make a difference in their life.

And then: Mira, are you there?

I came back to my phone and saw his messages.

Ehh, sorry. I went down to answer Popsi. He was calling me. You sound like my mother lol, I texted back.

It's true nau. Because of chop belleful, they start thinking they don't need God anymore. The average Nigerian is depending on God for their daily bread. By God's grace we keep surviving, and at the end of the day, we have reason to thank God.

So what does that have to do with mental health? I asked.

No, I'm just saying I think our resilience and religiousness help us not to have mental health issues. Somebody needs to do that research to see the connection between religiousness and mental health. You like research. Maybe you should do it.

Trust me, I'm sure it's been done before, and yes, we can't deny there is an important link between spirituality and better mental health. Notice I said spirituality, not religiousness. There is a difference.

Hmm. So which one do they have there?

I ignored the question and typed. So what will self-actualization look like for you?

Me? I just want a family I can be proud of and a job that pays well enough to buy a solar panel so that I will not be bothered by PHCN issues, Midowa texted back.

Lol very important, I responded.

What about you?

I have a fulfilling career with a doctorate, awards and accolades to my name making my parents proud when they think of me. I sat up and processed Midowa's comment. As Nigerians, it is true that our religiousness is the lens through which we see our experiences. Although it seemed that this created a barrier in furthering a scientific approach towards disability and mental health, it also provided a buffer for coping.

Midowa had start to respond and then deleted the message. He started to type again.

The third time around, the message finally came through.

Okay. I read the response. That should not have taken three minutes and three attempts to send. He was holding back.

That's not really what you want to say, is it? I texted and waited for a reply, picking the baby hairs at the nape of my neck.

Can you talk? Midowa responded.

Sure. As soon as I hit send, it seemed like he dialled immediately, the service miraculously giving a fast connection as if willing this conversation to happen.

"Hey," I answered cheerfully.

"Hey." His tone was flat, and I could guess why. It gave me a restless feeling, not just because I hated confrontation. Over the years as we went through countless phone calls, text messages, and video chats, we had argued about different things. Midowa had a strong personality, and I found myself withering whenever we disagreed.

"What's wrong?" I asked in the sweetest tone of voice I could muster.

"Samira," he said, using my full name, the first sign that the music had changed tune. "You said in your letter that you're still in, but I'm just wondering, do you really see me in your future?" I heaved a sigh and rolled my eyes up to the ceiling. I didn't have an answer for him, nor did I have the energy for a senseless fight.

I sighed. "Midowa, you realize that since I left Nigeria, now almost seven years I have been in this country, I have remained devoted to you, even though many guys have asked me out. Why do you think I am sticking with you if this is just for fun?"

"You didn't answer the question, Samira," he said almost immediately.

"Yes, Midowa, I see you in my future. That is why I have stayed with you, never giving attention to any of these other guys who want me, even the ones my parents have recommended. Unlike you, I have not dated anyone else since we came here." The last sentence flew out of my mouth with force.

Midowa breathed slowly. I was ready for him to shout or do whatever, but there were things that needed to be said. I had been avoiding it, but perhaps it was time.

"Samira, we were not talking for like a year."

"And you know that was because of all the things I had going on after moving here with getting admission to school and all that, but you knew I was still in. I just needed time to sort myself out."

"I know, and I promised you that I was not upset or anything. Do you realize that if I had not told you about it, you wouldn't have known about the girl?"

Silence.

"Midowa, I know you. I'm going to tell you now that I really believe I can trust you, and I appreciate you telling me about her. I know that it was a mistake. I mean, why else would you be talking to a girl studying marine science—like have you heard of mammy water before?"

I heard him scoff and thanked God the deflection was working.

"Midowa, I know you are good for me. Maybe that's why I'm comfortable, but please don't ever doubt that you are the one I want to annoy for the rest of my life."

"So you know you're comfortable. Anyway, sha don't be too comfortable because at some point I want to have a family, and I want it to be with you. But I will not force you if you're not ready to give it your all."

"Have you ever thought about where we would live?" I asked in a whisper. Midowa had said that my voice took on an annoying pitch when we argued.

"That doesn't matter to me." There was a finality to that comment that hit me like a sack of potatoes.

"Oh, it doesn't? Let's be realistic. Either of two things will have to happen for us to be together. One, you come here for school or work or whatever and stay here, or two, I move back to Nigeria. We have to face the reality that either of those options will require sacrifices that we have to start making now. So the truth is, I'm not the only one who is holding this back. You haven't really been doing anything about this yourself." I pulled the phone away from me to catch my breath after that long-winded retort.

Quiet.

"If you're saying you want me to abandon my life here to come home and marry you, then tell me that's what you want. Spell it out. At least we'll know that's the deal-breaker." The words kept coming out without a stutter, much to my surprise. I hoped that Dahdee could not hear any of this shouting on the phone. The TV was on downstairs, and as long as he did not come up, I could carry on.

"What if you come back and you're not happy here? How do you think I will be able to live with myself?" Now Midowa was the one whispering.

"What if you come here because of me and you hate it and then resent me?"

"So either way there is a chance that we may hate it. It definitely requires a sacrifice, but I guess that's the question: What are we willing to risk and at what cost?"

"Right, and that goes both ways." I added this last part with a neck roll.

"See, if I resent you, I think that will be more bearable than you resenting me. I can't even imagine that. I won't forgive myself." He paused. "But I guess that's the risk you have to take for what you want."

"Yeah. Honestly, it will be easier for you to just find somebody there and marry. I don't know if this will work."

He scoffed.

"Have you ever asked yourself if maybe the reason you never dated anyone else is because you're just afraid of relationships?"

"Well, I guess you've figured me out, so what then?" I felt my stomach start to knot.

Midowa sighed, and neither of us said anything for a while. "You know what you always tell me when I say I can never understand all these mental health issues?" he finally asked.

I was tempted to tell him that I would be coming home soon and we can sort things out. I hoped that if I really did go back, spending time together again would renew our commitment, and we would finally decide how to move forward.

"Try," he continued. "That's all we can do try. I learned from my parents that marriage is not perfect, but when two people are determined to stay together, they will always overcome."

"Yeah." *I learned from my parents that even when two people love each other, betrayal is inevitable* I thought but didn't say.

"Lemme leave you to sleep now," Midowa said after trying and failing to make small talk about irrelevant things.

"Hmm. Sleep ke. t's still early for me. You're the one who needs sleep sef." I failed in my attempt to sound casual.

"Okay now. Good night, babe." He sounded deflated. I realized that it was a mistake to leave Nigeria with the intention of continuing this relationship. We should have broken it off while it was simpler, unspoiled, and uncomplicated. Then we would have the contentment of what was.

"Good night." I ended the call and crashed into my pillow.

Chapter 10

ON THE WAY HOME

I left a voice mail on Aunty Silvia's phone to find out if she was still planning to go to Nigeria and got a call back four days later.

"Ah, my dear, I've been soo busy." I interjected phrases of understanding, rolling my eyes the whole time.

"I understand, Aunty. I just wanted to know when you'll be going to Nigeria again."

"Eeem, my dear, I'm not sure o, but I was looking at January."

"Ehn, ehn, okay, Aunty. I've decided to attend that program. I've been talking to Aunty Tolani, and she's been very helpful."

"Oh that's good!" I was shocked by how genuinely pleased she seemed.

She continued. "So when are you looking at? Because the program is in November. That's what, four months from now?"

"Yes, ma. I was planning to go maybe mid-October. That way, I have enough time to settle down. She sent me the volunteer form, and I filled it out, so I'm waiting to hear back from them."

"That's good. You're making moves. I like that, ehen. That's how it should be. What are your parents saying about it?"

"They are all right with it, just worried about me travelling back by myself."

Aunty Silvia laughed. "Ehn, that's understandable sha, but they should realize they need to let you mature on your own." I was always fascinated by the fact that Aunty Silvia and her husband never had any children. I was curious about the full story hoping that it would explain why she was so judgmental of whatever other people did with their own children.

"So you haven't bought your ticket yet?"

"No, Aunty. I wanted to check with you first to see if you were going around the same time. I know my parents would prefer that."

"Yeah, yeah. Ah, I was thinking of January o, but you know what? Lemme get back to you. Don't buy the ticket yet. Let me check some things, and I'll be in touch."

"Yes, Aunty. I'll wait to hear back from you. Thank you, ma!"

"Okay, my dear. Greet your mummy."

I hung up feeling my heart beating a little faster. What would be the chance that Aunty Silvia could actually go with me? That would be such a relief, as much as I hated to admit that I was even depending on it. I picked up my phone again to send Midowa a message and decided it was too soon to say anything. In fact, I would wait until it was close enough to the day to surprise him.

I walked over to the closet and looked at my clothes. I had taken trips with my parents within the US to visit friends, but I had not been anywhere international.

I needed to buy a new suitcase. *Nigeria, here I come!*

The thought of going back home after so long filled me with excitement and trepidation. Nayana was back in the States, and I commended her for sticking it out for a whole month. Much to my disappointment, she had not changed much. All I heard were complaints about how substandard and inconvenient everything was.

Girl, seriously, the skyline was so gloomy, I couldn't believe it was real life, with the rusted zinc roofs blending in with the colour of the sand!

Girl, y'all got like the inferno over here. It's soo hot!

Girl, what's with these police people and asking for handouts?

She had been too busy since getting back to come for a sleepover, so we decided to meet at Panera Bread early in August.

Walking up to the café to meet Nayana, I had a weird feeling in the pit of my stomach. It occurred to me that I still reserved some discomfort about Nayana's time with Midowa.

I had put on some foundation and eyeliner with coloured lip gloss, a recent development as I prepared to see Midowa again.

My mother had never approved of me wearing makeup. She had convinced me that it would suppress my natural beauty. She had even gone as far as telling me scary tales of people aging because of makeup. I was inclined to agree with her, as I had come to believe that lime poisoning had stunted my growth in childhood. Even though Aunty Zubaida had defied that executive order from Muhmee and encouraged me to do the same, I never felt the need to put on makeup. Perhaps because it was yet another opportunity to show my mother that I was in fact the good child and that Aunty Zubaida was a nightmare.

Until one day when we were going to a wedding and Muhmee asked me in the car, "Ahnahn, Samira. Why is your face like this, with no makeup?"

My eyes nearly popped out of my head as I gawked at my mother. The almighty Azeezat herself had been slipping in a liner here and a lip gloss there since she became a nurse. As if that was a way to confirm that her status had been upgraded.

"Muhmee, you know I don't wear makeup, thanks to you!" I had responded.

"Ehn, ehn, so it's that one that you listen to, but if I tell you now to stop touching my things, you will disobey me. Please take this lip gloss and put it on at least."

I had slathered on the ruby red lip gloss, shaking my head in disbelief and thinking how Nigerian parents wrote the book on doublespeak. They would skin you alive for talking to boys when you're in school but rebuke you for being an old maid years later.

Unbelievable.

"Hey, baby girl!" I called out to Nayana when I spotted her sitting in a booth. We hugged, and I squeezed her arms playfully, asking if she gained any weight from Nigeria.

"Girl, my aunt was legit force-feeding me. I couldn't keep up." She flipped the braids she had made before she left Nigeria.

"Aww, I'm sure she was happy you came. That was the first time you ever met her, right, and your cousins?"

Nayana told me how her little cousins followed her around all day and asked her questions. She said she missed them, but other than that, she didn't miss much else about Nigeria.

"At least I got tons of pictures for the competition. So far, the agama lizard is really popular. Those things were everywhere and so dramatic with their push-ups."

"So what did you think of Midowa?" I tried to sound casual, taking a bite of my blueberry scone.

"He was really nice, tuh. His one friend was trying so hard to get my attention, but he wasn't cute."

"So none of the guys you met interested you?" I watched her face closely.

"I mean, some of them were cool, but there was too much going on. I was having a hard time settling down." She appeared to be avoiding my face. I studied her body language and noticed that something had actually changed. There was a certain way that her head moved when she talked. Nigeria had definitely rubbed off on her.

"Hmm. So would you date Midowa if he was single?" I added, feeling Nayana get tense.

"Are you seriously asking me that?" Her mouth flew open, and it seemed like her eyeballs were bouncing in her head.

"Ahnahn, I'm joking now." I laughed to make things light, but the look on Nayana's face gave me instant regret.

"I'm just saying girls usually like him, so—"

"Samira, lemme ask you something," she cut in. "What do you think would have happened if I had been a different kind of girl and had fallen in love with your man?"

"I know you're not that kind of girl. I was just teasing. Anyway, Midowa would probably not have even been interested."

Nayana scoffed. "Yeah, well, don't test that theory, because like you said, Lagos girls are too sharp. They will take him from right under you, missy." She picked up a piece of toast and buttered it a little too zealously. "All I'm saying is that guy adores you. You want my opinion? You either claim him or cut him loose."

I blinked, my mind swirling with conflicting thoughts. I could not believe how stern Nayana was being with me. That had never happened before. I opened my mouth to confess that I had suspected something was going on between them, to appeal to her for one last honest answer so that I could finally put the matter to rest.

"Did you just say too sharp?" I scoffed, shaking my head. Maybe another day I would have the courage to ask her again. Maybe not ever. Maybe it didn't matter.

"Girl, blame my cousins. I've been speaking like them since I got back."

"Correct, they did their job." I watched her mindlessly chewing away and decided that there was nothing to worry about. I chose to trust that Nayana was not that kind of girl and that our friendship was important to her. Besides, Midowa clearly was not interested in looking at any other girl. Whether I was right about those two things, time would tell.

"I'm going to Nigeria in two months oo." I had waited to tell her just in case she and Midowa were still in touch.

"Wow, okay. That's random! Does Midowa know?"

"Yeah, I just told him. I actually wanted to surprise him but decided it wasn't worth the risk to tell him at the last minute." There was so much to coordinate.

"Ha, interesting. How long are you staying?" I couldn't stop smiling as Nayana spoke in almost fluent Naija.

"Over a month. Why interesting?"

"I told Midowa you would try to surprise him whenever you decide to come. Guess I know you better than you know me." She rolled her neck and pouted her mouth.

"Ehn, I hear. You're my mother ni."

"Cool. So are you going to do that program thingy?"

"Yeah. I just got approved to volunteer, so when I settle down, I'll be working with one of the professionals from here to organize things and do an outreach in the community."

"Nice. Would you consider working there?"

"In Nigeria? Eemm, I dunno. It depends. If I get a job offer, I'll see if it's worth it."

"Tuh, workers in Nigeria are funny. They seemed to be more interested in performing than in actually doing their jobs. Like they just wanna wear suits and look important; meanwhile, they have no qualifications whatsoever," she spat, shaking her head.

Ordinarily I would have been offended by that comment, but I quietly agreed. Nayana was not the same person she was before she went to Nigeria. Whether she recognized it or not, she had acquired a level of knowing by being there. I couldn't wait to see how she would manifest it.

As my trip to Nigeria drew closer, my parents kept asking if I was sure about going. The more they raised objections, the more convinced I became that I needed to go. I suddenly felt like it was a very important thing I was doing—important and urgent.

Muhmee reminded me of some of the crazy experiences we had in Lagos before coming to the US.

"Ah, remember that day I wanted to kill that okada man?" She shook her head and sucked her teeth.

"Ah, Dahdee, you should have seen it. Mummy turned into Rambo." I watched Muhmee's face take on an odd angle, like she was hot stuff. Dahdee had heard the story before, but I doubt that he ever got the full weight of the kinds of things Muhmee endured in his absence.

We were on our way back from Dr. Godwin's house, and Muhmee and I hardly spoke. Any question I asked had been met with a grunt. Like me, Muhmee appeared to be lost in thought, processing the visit with the doctor and his wife. I had school the next day and worried about getting caught in the usual Lagos traffic. I could not wrap my head around what had possessed Muhmee to bring me out on a school night to visit this peculiar couple with no children. To me, adults in all their wisdom seemed to always make the most juvenile decisions for God knows what reason.

It was around 8:30p.m. when we left the couple's house, which thankfully was not too late to get to bed for school the next day.

As I wandered through the depths of my mind to sort out my discovery at the doctor's house, I felt the car jerk in my direction as Muhmee screamed out, "God!" The tires screeched to a halt on the motorway, with cars honking and weaving to get past us. A motorcyclist somehow emerged from the corner of Muhmee's window, screaming abuses at her.

"Madam, you dey crase. You no see as I dey come?" he barked, spit flying everywhere.

"Me? Are you mad? You didn't see that I was dodging the pothole over here? Are you mad?" Muhmee retorted.

"Me, mad ke. You will know who is mad now!"

The man had turned around, and as Muhmee went to start the car, lamenting the disgrace of motorcyclists as an endangerment to society, I heard a loud crash followed by shards of glass showering me. Muhmee and I screamed. I opened my eyes, and as I was about to ask Muhmee what had happened, the motorcyclist revved his engine and sped off.

"Are you okay?" Muhmee asked me, the maddening look of fear widening her eyes.

"Yes, Mum." I breathed heavily. "What . . ."

Muhmee started the car and screeched back onto the road. It took a moment for me to realize that she was chasing the bike man, her head moving from side to side and her eyes burning.

"Muhmee?"

She was muttering threats under her breath, and I knew there was no backing down.

I perked up in my seat and started searching and pointing. "Muhmee, I think that's him!" My eyes began to water. I couldn't tell if it was tears or something the man had thrown at us. All I knew was that now he was going to pay.

The traffic was light, and cars were speeding on. I panicked that Muhmee was driving too close to them. I suddenly realized that I didn't know what the man looked like or what he had on. It didn't help that there were other motorcyclists on the same route, weaving in chaotic harmony. But Muhmee seemed sure of her target, so I kept looking, intent on helping her bring the man to justice. As I fixed my eyes on a bike man who I was convinced was him speeding ahead, Muhmee sharply turned the corner into a busy street. *Okay, not him. She must know the right man then*, I thought. The busy roads were full of people selling, and in all that bustling, I couldn't believe the speed with which Muhmee was going about the chase.

Next thing I knew, Muhmee used the iron bumper of her Rodeo Jeep to knock over the bike man. My eyes grew in disbelief.

"Muhmee, did you just hit him?"

She jumped out of the car and grabbed the man by his shirt, bellowing in pure rage how dead he was going to be. I also jumped out, partly in the hope that I could somehow prevent my mother from ripping the man apart. Truly the man did not know who he was messing with. My mother's rage was enough any day to take down man, woman, or deity. Suddenly Muhmee stopped shaking the man, who was now calling out, "Ahnahn, madam! Wetin I do?"

She took slow breaths and peered into the man's face, realization dawning that she had hit the wrong bike man. She shoved him to the ground and rushed back to the car.

"Samira, let's go!" I flew into the car, amazed by my mother's reticence in this wildly exciting and insanely dangerous saga. Muhmee screeched off, leaving the bike man and a concerned crowd who had gathered to help him, probably wondering what in the world she was on. She whipped the car around and got back onto the main road, her head darting desperately in all directions—front, side, and behind. Finally, she pulled to the side of the road and slammed her palm on the wheel in defeat.

Oh God! I searched around and concluded that the bike man was now long gone. Our chase had come to an unaccomplished end.

What exactly was Muhmee planning to do to that bike man? I couldn't help wondering.

I felt a rush of emotion as I heard her say, "With a child in the car, ehn. What if-if-if he had wounded her?" Muhmee always stuttered when she was especially aggravated.

"Muhmee, I'm okay. Let's go home." She looked over at me, eyes brimming with revenge as her chest rose and fell. I touched her arm. "Mummy, it's all right. Let's go."

She hissed and shook her head. "Okay." She was not satisfied, but she conceded.

We met some light traffic on the way back but thankfully made it home before long. Not much else was said during the ride except for Muhmee shouting her own name and shaking her head as if calling on history to come view what had become of her. "Azeezat, Azeezat. Zee! Kai!" And that would be followed by *mene ne wannan*—what rubbish!

When she was dressed up to go out, Azeezat Ofunwa was exquisite to look at. She had put on her best that evening, raising my suspicion about where we were going. With ankle-length Ankara dresses and her hair wrapped in the same fabric, she would throw on a silk scarf over her head, and it would fall ever so lightly over her. "Madam Zee!" the neighbourhood guys would hail her as she floated towards her car, gold watch and rings glinting in the sun and handbag in the crook of her arm. Her regal form appeared delicate with her smallish frame and baby face. Only those who knew her were not at all fooled by her sweetness.

As the altercation unfolded with the bike man, I thought how unbefitting the outfit seemed as she cursed and ranted about all that was wrong with the country. "These useless okada people should all be gathered and thrown into the bush!" Her venom against them was valid, as there had been countless occasions when we almost got hit by one of them.

"Ehn, imagine, imagine!" Muhmee lamented well into our arrival at home. Aunty Zubaida had asked what happened and was told to give Muhmee a glass of water and fill her a bucket for a bath.

Truly there were things that Dahdee would never grasp about his time away from us. The event that took place earlier that evening, even before the bike man chase, was one that I couldn't bear to recall. I was sure that Muhmee had never told Dahdee about it.

"See if Eniola will go with you to see Mama, abeg. Don't go alone," Muhmee urged me at dinner, excited that I would be going to visit my grandma in Kano but understandably worried.

"Yes, Mum," I responded. We were all gathered in the living room with Aunty Zubaida, who was visiting. Muhmee and Dahdee were always as excited as I was to see her. Muhmee kept fussing that she did not look good, and Aunty Zubaida talked about the stress she was going through at work since her colleagues quit.

"These people, ehn, so annoying. They don't just want to work walahi *hiss*," she complained. I never did tell my parents about the recent crisis she had, as I promised. Noticing how off-colour she looked, though, I wondered if I should have.

"When did you last take vacation time?" Dahdee asked.

"Hmm, it's been long o. With all this overtime, they won't even answer me if I ask them."

"Well, health first. You have to do it one way or another. Tell them it's a medical emergency if you have to."

"Yes, Dahdee," Aunty Zubaida responded. I looked around the room, happy that we were all together again. How far we had come, all of us now in America as a unit, knowing the collective struggle it took. But we still had family in Nigeria, and I couldn't help thinking how much I was missing out on by not being connected to them. I wondered what Aunty Zubaida thought about me going home to see Grandma Ufi. I wished that somehow their relationship would be repaired and that they would realize how much they needed each other. Muhmee couldn't stop smiling as I told Grandma Ufi over the phone that I would be visiting. It amazed me that Muhmee was one person who loved her mother unconditionally and wanted her to be happy above all else.

Too bad Aunty Zubaida never got the chance to cultivate that kind of love for her.

We ate and reminisced about times in Nigeria and the crazy things we see in America. Aunty Zubaida finally left to get some sleep for work the next day.

I was awakened to a disturbance around four that morning and left my room to see what was going on.

"Zubaida is in the ER ooo. I said it, ehn. I said it!" As we all scrambled to get dressed and pile into the car to go the hospital, Muhmee, crying her eyes out, kept repeating, "I said it. Something was not right."

Chapter 11

OSONDU

I had spent so much time anticipating Aunty Zubaida's next crisis that I felt cheated by the time it happened. They were more frequent when we were younger, and the few times she ended up hospitalized, I was too small to even imagine that she could not pull through. Sitting at her hospital bedside, I watched her sleeping with IVs going through her, angry that life had teased the possibility that I had worried her condition away. That somehow the cumulative events she had been through, along with the ones I had conjured up in my mind, had met her quota.

It was not only her sickle cell anaemia I had to contend with. There was the one occasion when a nationwide crisis had me convinced I had lost her. It was the day of the Ikeja bomb blast after Muhmee and I had made it back home from visiting her in boarding school.

27 January 2002.

Early that evening Muhmee and I had gone to Aunty Zubaida's visiting day in boarding school. I was so excited; I had missed my aunt even though I knew I would regret that thought the minute school was out for the term.

"Bye-bye, smallie!" Aunty Zubaida had smacked my head as she swaggered off to join her friends. The visit had been hurried; she claimed she had to finish some homework for class the next day. I doubted that was the case, imagining that there was some exciting event that she needed to be at. On the ride home, I watched the passing cars quietly, my head resting on the window. I couldn't shake a strange feeling as I replayed the scene in my head—Aunty Zubaida walking away and suddenly what seemed like a thousand birds flying overhead. The air had changed, and the school quickly seemed to be quieter.

Something bad will happen to her. A strong inkling had convinced me that the miserable feeling I had was more than just disappointment that she had rushed off before I had even gotten a chance to rememorize her face.

The earth suddenly started to rumble in the midst of usual Lagos traffic, and I shot up in my seat, clutching my thumping chest. My first impossible thought as I searched Muhmee's face for assurance was that an earthquake had missed its route and nestled in the Nigerian earth. Next thing I knew, Muhmee was parking on the side of the road as chaos erupted all around us. The sound of glass shattering in the distance and a frantic woman screaming, "Bomb blast!" had me questioning reality. There was nowhere to go. Muhmee rushed me out of the car. "Come out!" she ordered, her voice shaking as she murmured prayers.

Somehow we ended up under the car just as a crowd of people broke out of every corner running helter-skelter. By this point, I was huddled so close to Muhmee under our Jeep that I could smell the fear on her breath, both of us with our eyes shut, hoping and praying for the terrorism to pass over us. Cramped and shivering in fear, I wondered if staying put was the best course of action. Didn't we need to run too, away from what appeared to be the direction of the danger?

Every true born Nigerian knows that when chaos erupts anywhere in your vicinity and you see a mass of people running, you run with them.

No questions asked.

Nigerians were a discerning group and could smell danger from a mere thought. There never were a people who loved their life more and who would flee from danger so as not to meet the same fate as the curious cat.

Osondu, Dahdee called it in his Igbo language. To run for one's life.

That day, osondu had caused some six hundred people to run into a hyacinth-filled canal in their bid to find safety. Someone in the general vicinity of the Oke-Afa Canal, which was a distance from the site of the explosion, realizing that something grave had taken over the city, probably rallied his family to run towards the banana fields on the other side to be safe. That easily, a crowd could have joined them in this run, growing in number of people who did not know where, nor could they even *see* where they were going in the darkness of the night. The crowd, possibly now over a thousand people who could have remained alive and well if they had sheltered in place, eventually rushed into the unsuspecting canal to an untimely death. The number of those who died in the actual bomb blast was about a mean of those who had drowned in the canal camouflaged as night. Add to that others around the city who had been caught under the feet of a stampede or bludgeoned by falling houses.

When it was safe to get back in the car, Muhmee drove like a madwoman until we reached our compound. The neighbourhood was full of chattering and hushed voices commenting over radio announcements and sharing theories. I sat in a corner by the gate as Muhmee caught up with the neighbours who had come out when they too felt the building shiver.

As the adrenaline started to wear off, I jumped to my feet, realizing that the eerie feeling I had when Aunty Zubaida said goodbye was still there.

"Mummy, when will you call Aunty Zubaida's school?" I ran to her side, frantic.

It was the next day before we could get any updates that the students in the school were safe. That was a mournful day in the neighbourhood. The usually boisterous greetings had become extraordinarily placating as people tried to process the event.

It would come to be called Black Sunday.

Neighbours swapped horror stories of where they had been when the tragedy hit. Most seemed to have been on their way to or back from church. They attributed this to their safety, the fact that they had paid their religious dues as the chaos unfolded. Surely the majority who had died had somehow failed in that regard.

Later, when Aunty Zubaida came home for the school break, she shared with me how she had experienced that event. She and her classmates, feeling the rumbling of the earth, had scattered in all directions, running around crying, "Coup in Nigeria! War! War!" She told me how images from movies like *Sarafina* had come into her head as they became more convinced that they were experiencing in their own lifetime some sort of military takeover. Yet in the chaos, they had found time to swap food from visiting day and fantasize about how they could be the heroes of a historic event. One minute they were worrying about how their parents were faring as the war unfolded, and the next minute they were making plans for the possibility that aside from any danger to them or their families, they would have a valid excuse to be out of school for some time.

It was a marvel how my aunt and her friends made light of that whole situation. While I tossed and turned in bed that night, my stomach churning in despair, Aunty Zubaida and her friends made fun, finding a silver lining to the frightening event.

Please, God, let her pull through, I prayed, touching her leg lightly.

"Smallie?" Aunty Zubaida had roused, her voice groggy from medication-induced sleep.

"Yes, Aunty Zubaida?"

"Please give me water." I ran out to the nurses' station and asked where I could find water. They directed me to the break room, where I filled a cup and hurried back to the room.

"How are you feeling?" I touched her neck to see if it was warm, as if that would tell me anything.

"I'm okay." Aunty Zubaida's voice was stronger after a drink.

"Muhmee and Dahdee left when the doctor told them you were stable."

"And you stayed. Don't you have work today?" I was being scolded for showing concern.

"I called my supervisor and explained the situation." I noticed that I was breathing fast as relief washed over me to see her awake.

"Hmm, oya. Go home and sleep now. I feel fine."

I was exhausted. My parents and I had been at my aunt's side right from the ER until they admitted her into a room. I had assured my parents that she would be okay and convinced them to go home. Muhmee only left when she called her job and they could not find someone else to work her shift. I watched my aunt, now picking up her phone and adjusting herself to sit upright. I knew she meant for me to leave. She did not like people doting on her and showing pity. I thought that there had to be a point when my aunt felt cheated in life, when she longed for someone to hold her, caressing her head and telling her that things would be all right. There had to be a point when she wished that person would be her mother.

"Ahnahn, what's wrong with this one?" Aunty Zubaida asked, seeing that my eyes were watering. I shook my head casually and wiped my cheeks. I felt winded, like hands were clutching at my windpipe from inside. I offered a slight smile and made peace with the fact that Aunty Zubaida was in a constant state of osondu with her illness. Unlike those people who died on that Black Sunday, though, she so far managed to outrun death. Just as she always seemed to crawl out of any hole that life threw her in, laughing off the sheer hilarity of it, she would get out of this one until next time.

As if to confirm that, Aunty Zubaida said, "Please, are Muhmee and Dahdee coming back? Because my boyfriend is coming to see me."

Ms. Rhonda summoned me into her office the next day after Aunty Zubaida's crisis.

As I walked over to her detached quarters, I found my mind wandering back to Nigeria and of Midowa and Nayana spending time together. That heavy sense of homesickness I felt when Nayana left was lifting as I planned my return back home. All of the vicarious enjoyment that I had tapped from her visit was about to become reality.

"Come in," I heard Ms. Rhonda call as I knocked on her door.

I walked into the familiar office that was as sterile as the first day I entered for an interview. The aesthetic didn't particularly strike me as odd. I was always more interested in what Ms. Rhonda had to say than in the fact that there was never a pot of candy sitting on her table, as my co-workers always pointed out in disgust. She had pictures of her family on her desk, but my co-workers hated that there was no flower vase and other lavish decoration typical in most managers' offices. As they ranted on about how her cold office was akin to her manner, I couldn't help but wonder why the look of her work space was so important. I told them that overdecorated offices seemed to me like the person was trying too hard to relate. I liked that this office was sterile, as they termed it. This woman was clearly not trying to make an impression. Whatever you wanted from her you would get in organic doses straight out of her mouth or by the look in her eyes. Perhaps it was on purpose that she kept her office so nondescript, or perhaps the woman doesn't know the first thing about decorating. In any case, the content of her office would only be discussion among my American counterparts. What Nigerian would be paying attention to the decoration in someone's work space?

Ms. Rhonda motioned me to a chair and positioned herself in hers.

"How's it going?"

"It's going well, ma'am." A small smile flashed across her face at that term. I knew what she was thinking. I tried so hard to get out of calling her Ms. Kurst, as I did in the beginning. She had insisted that I call her by first name, and I vehemently refused, pleading with her to understand how inappropriate it was in my culture. Nayana had told me before that white people don't care about that formality as much as Black people do, so if the woman said to call her by her first name, then just do it. Then I decided it would be Ms. Rhonda, reducing the Ms. to a whisper and then exaggerating the Rhonda. So it ended up sounding like Sronda.

She would chuckle every time I said it, and although I wished she would just get over it, she always pointed out that it would be a sign of respect to call her by a preferred term, which in this case is her first name.

"Ehn!" The expression flew out of my mouth before I knew it.

Calling her by name a sign of respect! How?

The dialogue with my inside voice would start back up anytime I was speaking with her. I was determined to respond to her with a *ma'am* no matter what, before my ancestors will be rolling in their graves.

"That's good." Ms. Rhonda nodded and let silence hang in the air for a minute. I realized for the first time that the lack of any decorations in the office was indeed unnerving. At that very moment, I would have commented on a painting or some other welcome distraction to avert the woman's gaze.

I looked over at the single piece of decor: a family picture with her two sons, who looked to be not quite as white as their parents.

"How is your family?" I suppressed a smile, remembering multiple times in my childhood when my mother had drilled it into my brain to ask about family when speaking to adults.

"But, Mummy, what should I ask them?" I would whine.

"Can't you ask about their family?"

Yes, a good child always asked adults about their family. In Nigeria it showed concern and was an excellent icebreaker. In America it seemed invasive and weird.

"My family's doing well, thanks for asking." Ms. Rhonda smiled genuinely.

Good, she doesn't think it's strange.

She continued. "That's Carlos and Jeremy, my babies. They're eleven—"

"Aww, twins!" I kept looking at the photo.

"Adopted actually."

"Oooooh ookayyyyy!" It finally registered in my brain. Ms. Rhonda and her husband were *white* white, but the boys seemed more coloured. In all the years I lived in the States, I still couldn't tell for sure if a light-skinned person was white or Hispanic or even Black. To me they were all oyibo. I learned to keep my ignorance to myself so as not to offend but secretly wondered why there's a wide spectrum of Black but not white.

"Nice. Wow," I offered, wondering what the full story was. Could she not have children of her own, or did she just want to help out some kids in need?

"Samira, I wanted to check in with you to see how you were finding things and to discuss next steps. You've been here for how long now?"

"Four months," I responded.

"Already? It flew by. Four months, huh? Well, you've come a long way since then, I must say. I remember when you first came here; you were definitely a fish out of water. You would flinch every time one of the kids had an outburst."

My eyes turned down. It was true; I used to get startled by every movement. In all honesty, I still was not really used to it all, the spitting, the crises that would require restraints, and interpreting the unusual communication cues.

As if reading my mind, Ms. Rhonda continued. "I can tell it's still hard for you. I was watching you the other day when Eric was trying to hold your hand in the group." She laughed and mimicked Eric's voice asking me to clasp his hand properly.

"He can be pretty intense." She cocked her head in commiseration. "We'like be coming up on six months soon. What are your plans afterwards?" she suddenly added.

"I'm trying to get an idea of what to do my master's in and then I'll apply to school and maybe work part-time. I'm actually going back home in October for a program. I think that will really help me find my focus."

"What's the program about?"

"It's an autism awareness program sponsored by a bank in Nigeria. They had done one last year, and another one is coming this year. They are trying to do it annually."

"That's interesting. Are there many such programs in your home country?"

"Not that I've ever heard of. That's why I want to go and see what it's like. I've been speaking with a contact who is involved with the program, and she said they're gonna have behavioural analysts onsite for evaluation. It seems to be getting some good response so far."

"That's very exciting. So when is the program starting exactly and for how long?"

"It's on the fourth of November, and it will be for two days."

Ms. Rhonda nodded, looking me up and down. She drew a breath.

"I think you should do it. It's a great thing to bring such awareness to your home country in Africa. Kevin and I did some work in Malawi and Kenya. Best experience of our lives. Now I imagine the culture might be a bit of a barrier from what I know about Nigeria, but it's worth jumping on that ship before it sails."

"Yes, ma'am." I twiddled my fingers.

"Well, keep me posted when you get back. You should think about applying here. I see something good in you, and I appreciate your professionalism and conscientiousness. I would hire you based on that."

"Based on that?" I asked, wondering if a compliment or a critique was coming.

Deep breath.

"Samira, you have a good nature about you, I can tell. I can also tell that you care about this population of kids with behavioural issues. But you're holding back. You're not comfortable in this space yet, and until you can fully embrace it, you'll get burned out and quit. This is not a field one goes into for the money, right? It's for the heart. You still have to do a lot of self-work and make sure that this is where you really want to be."

I felt like I was being told off and would have burst into tears in a second.

Ms. Rhonda saw the look on my face. "You'll be fine. I know many people who join this field to do some kind of penance, and they often don't get it." She swivelled her chair from side to side. "You see this office?" She motioned about the room.

"There's a reason why I keep it boring. There's a lot of trauma in the population we work with and by that I don't mean just the kids but also the staff. I'm fully aware of that, and the last thing I would want to do is retraumatise anyone by my own actions. I don't know where everyone has been or what they're struggling with, so I decided to create a safe space without any potential triggers. That's how you think in this field—think of yourself and your environment as a vessel to hold someone safely, not a vessel to retraumatise. This is more than a job, Samira. It's a mindset, and it's a way of life. I take nothing for granted, even my clothes. I put some thought into it as a potential vessel. I've heard the whispers about how I'm dressed too seriously, but just think if my outfit was provocative and I was interacting with someone who's experienced sexual trauma. What do you think would happen? I've actually seen it occur. Not good."

"Right." I nodded as the gravity of what she said sank in. It occurred to me that one of my co-workers must have said something about me.

"Don't worry. It'll come more naturally to you with time. I just want you to remember this"—she raised a finger, her nails unpolished but well manicured—"get comfortable being uncomfortable. Throw yourself out of your comfort zone and find a new comfort zone. Trust me. I know it's hard in this field, and boy, I have to take a few drinks some nights. But you have to reset and show up."

"Yes, ma'am."

"All right. Like I said, keep me posted. Maybe we can invite you as a guest speaker to share your experience."

"Yes, ma'am. I really appreciate your feedback." My voice croaked.

I started to rise out of my seat but hesitated.

"Anything else?" she asked.

"Um, actually, I've been meaning to ask—it's just something I was thinking about."

"Yes?"

I coughed and perked my shoulders up. "How do the parents of these kids feel about our restraining practices?" I tried to sound as academic as I could manage.

She nodded slowly, examining me as if deciding how diplomatic her answer should be.

"Hmm, that's a tough one. I imagine they don't like it. But they certainly understand that it's necessary. I think a few of them even use it in their homes."

"Really?"

"Yes. We've trained parents to do it safely at home, especially where there is a threat to siblings."

"I see."

"What do they use in your home country to manage threatening behaviours?" Her eyes suddenly seemed to throw icicles at me.

"You know what, I don't know. I'd have to ask when I get there."

"Yes, you should. I can't imagine it would be much different. I mean, Africans historically had some very inhuman practices around mental health."

"That's true, but I hear things are changing now," I fired back, feeling my neck roll.

"Well, I would be very happy if you could share that with us when you return."

"Yes, ma'am," I responded firmly.

Chapter 12

RECONNECTING

When departure day came, I felt my stomach grumble on the way to the airport, like the intestinal bag had dropped right down to my anus, ready to burst out. I was excited and nervous, hopeful and anxious. I was not looking forward to the flight but thanked God that Aunty Silvia, as annoying as always, would be there with me. We had arranged to meet at the airport. She arrived in a taxi by herself while I came with my parents, my aunt, and Nayana.

"Ahnahn, Samira. You brought a whole convoy with you, Princess Samira," Aunty Silvia teased and tapped me on the back. I smiled and decided that for the benefit of her company on the plane ride, I would not let the woman get to me. I couldn't deny how profound a sacrifice she had made to change her travel plans to accommodate me. I knew it was because Muhmee had likewise done more than enough for her in the past. Still, I was thankful and told her every chance I got.

"It's okay, my dear. What are family friends for?" she replied modestly. We had our bags checked and got our boarding passes.

I hugged everyone goodbye and joked with Nayana that it felt like déjà vu.

Aunty Silvia and I walked through security and then, one hour and thirty minutes later, we took off to Washington, DC, where we would pick up our connecting flight.

When the plane lifted into the air, I clenched through that horrible sensation of falling through space, dragging my body against gravity to balance itself. That was only my second flight ever, after the first one to the US. I struggled to get comfortable, to fall asleep, to enjoy the dreamy sight of clouds floating by, but nothing could pacify my flight anxiety.

Finally, the tires hit the tarmac, and a round of applause exploded, most appropriately, I thought.

Chatter started. People were obviously as sick of the plane as I was. Passengers began getting out of their seats as the plane rolled to a stop. They too could not wait to get out and get on with their reunions. I unbuckled my seat belt hurriedly, anxious to get away from the leery guy beside me who had tried the whole flight to start a conversation. He seemed determined to get one last word in to extend the episode of our paths crossing on that flight. I grabbed my hand luggage from the overhead bin. Slowly people finally made their way onto the passenger boarding bridge to the airport terminal. As I stepped onto the bridge, I noticed that the air had shifted to a certain coarseness coated with a musty smell. I wanted to smile, to embrace the wonderful feeling of being back home, but this home seemed like it belonged to someone else. The dimness of the room was so unfamiliar, I couldn't remember it being that dull when we were leaving. It looked like someone was casting a shadow over the lighting as my eyes suddenly dropped in sensitivity. I picked up my steps to keep up with Aunty Silvia, vwho was marching with purpose.

People were chattering in Yoruba as well as in the very Nigerian English. My senses were all over the place, equally excited and startled. So much was filtering through my head as I searched for overhead signs directing us to immigration. I found none. I noticed everyone, including Aunty Silvia, picking up their pace and thumping on the concrete floor like they knew where to go. I drew back to follow behind her. As we approached the moving walkway, I noticed why no one was going on it: It was not moving. We got to the escalator stairs going down where people had stopped, because that too was not moving. Wondering what was going on, I looked ahead and saw that there was a long line backed up all the way to the last stair.

This was what Nayana complained about, I thought, and for once she was not exaggerating. I was increasingly feeling disappointment over the inefficiency of this welcome back home.

People were starting to shed their luggage, and I was glad I had only a handbag and my neck pillow to carry. My heart started to beat faster as the human barricade did not budge. I rolled my neck to relieve the strain, and just then I noticed a sign overhead. My light T-shirt had started to cling to my irritated skin as my arm hair tingled in shock. The sign read:

WELCOME TO NIGERIA

HOME OF THE HAPPIEST PEOPLE ON EARTH

I studied the sign for a moment. My eyes dropped to scan the crowd of people crunched up in line in front of me. Multiple items had been converted to hand fans, as the air-conditioning was barely working. Heads shifted irritably to find a comfortable resting position as the wait continued. I looked back up at the sign and pulled out a hair bobble to restrain my braids into a high bun. I rubbed the back of my neck, fantasizing about diving into a pool or sinking into an ice bath or taking a decent shower at least. I closed my eyes, feeling the tension relieve as the rubbing relaxed me. I didn't want to reunite with Midowa looking stressed. I opened my eyes with a loud exhale only to find a young man at the bottom of the escalator staring at me. I fixed my eyes again on the queue, feeling a pang of guilt at that exaggerated display of discomfort.

Without warning, the lights went off. In that temporary moment of darkness, I paused to reorient myself, remembering how I had prepared Nayana for power outages in Nigeria. There I was taken by surprise as it dawned on me that it could happen even at the airport. As I made to turn around, squinting in the darkness to find some mysterious explanation, the power came back on. Hands formed into a round of applause that started small and then grew, coupled with laughs and indistinct commentary. The flash of the dim lights coming back on shocked my eyes into readjusting to what was nothing more than a tease of brightness. I took low deep breaths to calm my raging senses, and as the humid air expanded in my nose, I prayed I wouldn't pass out. I took a cue from Aunty Silvia, who joined in the applause and tapped my shoulder, shouting, "Welcome home!"

We finally got through immigration and walked out to baggage claim. I took shameless pride in the fact that I had gone through the foreigner line while Aunty Silvia went through the national. I flaunted my American accent, thrilled that the moment had finally arrived, the one that I had imagined since I first heard we would be moving to the States. It was the moment when I would come back to the same worshipful eyes that I had left envying me for going to America, the effizy that would cloud me as a returnee from abroad. I would open my mouth and people would hear my tinted accent, and for that reason alone, I would be a hotcake without further need to impress. I wished Aunty Zubaida was there with me. She certainly would have made a spectacle of herself in the way that arrogant Nigerians do when they come home.

While I savoured the debut of my American coolness, I couldn't help feeling disappointed by what I saw of the airport we had once flown out of. There were renovations going on in every corner, and although the airport was never quite the Taj Mahal in my memory, the tatters I saw were extremely unfamiliar. This landing in Lagos turned out to be not as magnificent as I had pictured, and I wanted to go back for a do-over. Porters flocked around Aunty Silvia and me, asking to bring us a cart and take our bags. Aunty Silvia shushed them and effortlessly went over to a counter, paid some money, and wheeled one to the conveyor belt.

"These people will take all your money if you answer them," she said to me. I didn't realize I was clinging to her, hanging on to every word like a sheep tired from escaping wild animals. Somehow all the effizy I had saved up in America seemed to have departed between the plane ride and the hectic arrival.

"Make call, make call." Some people standing around the building exit sang out as we walked through customs. I adjusted myself and checked my breath, making sure I was at my best to see Midowa. I felt flustered. For all my pride as a Naija girl, the chaotic airport scene left me feeling quite out of place.

"You said your friend is coming to pick you?" Aunty Silvia asked.

"Yes, Aunty. He will take me to my aunty's house in Surulere."

"Ehn, ehn, okay. Do you want to call him?"

"Okay, ma." I collected Aunty Silvia's phone and dialled Midowa's number.

"Hello?" his voice answered, questioning.

"Hey, Midowa. It's me. We're heading outside now. Are you here?"

He shouted, "My baby has landed!" I hoped that Aunty Silvia could not hear him. I did not want her to know anything about this "friend."

"I'm outside. Just be coming." He sounded like he was walking.

"Okay. See you in a bit." I handed back the phone.

As the sliding doors opened, we were greeted with a gust of hot, damp wind. I saw a sea of people searching faces that exited to welcome their own person. I turned slightly and saw Midowa pulling himself up from picking something off the ground.

He ran towards me and lifted me up, swinging me around until I could barely see. As he squeezed my back, I sniffed him and remembered how back in the day, the breaths I took greedily of him were the sweetest. I melted into him, conscious of the grime and sweat from the humid airport and of Aunty Silvia's eyes.

I heard Aunty Silvia chuckle and begged for Midowa to put me down.

"Ah, Mummy. Good evening, ma. Welcome, ma." Midowa bowed and touched his feet, his face betraying the lie that he was just a friend to me.

"Ehen, my dear. How are you? Hey, Samira, your friend is a handsome boy. Oh, hmm. Are you sure he's just a friend?" Aunty Silvia teased.

I mustered the most innocent smile that my tired face could manage.

"Mummy, where is your car? Is somebody picking you up?" Midowa asked like the woman was the reason he was there.

"No, my dear. I'll charter a cab at the car park."

"Okay, ma. Lemme get this for you." He grabbed the cart that had our bags, all the while staring at me with a sheepish smile plastered on his face.

"How was the flight?" he asked and looked over at Aunty Silvia.

"Ah, it was good o. Just the flight from DC was bumpy chei., Samira was so scared," she responded with a laugh.

"Hmm, Aunty. Seriously, thank God you were there. If not, I would have been squeezing some stranger's hand." Truly I was thankful the woman was sitting beside me and assuring me that the bumps were normal. Of course she found a way to inject comments about how a frequent flyer like her knows how to get comfortable.

"Oga, you dey go? Mummy, what's your address, ma?" Midowa bargained with the taxi man to get a good price to take Aunty Silvia. I watched the exchange, thinking how older women in Nigeria get the best out of the young men whose chivalry only existed in the presence of a woman they considered old enough to be their mother. It was stunning.

"Thank you, my dear. Please take her home o and be safe. Samira, call me, okay?" Aunty Silvia called out to us as the taxi drove off.

Midowa held my hand and planted a kiss on my cheek.

"Wow, Samira. Is this really you?" I felt my face flush, intimidated by his intense gaze.

He opened the car door and let me in. I was certain the chivalrous display was only for the novelty of our reunion and knew better than to expect it again.

He hopped into the car and looked at me again, his teeth sparkling in delight.

"Na wa o, why are you looking at me like TV?" I asked, shoving his arm.

"My dear, you are my TV for today. Wow, six years, Samira!"

"Yeah, wow. Naija seems to have changed so much."

"Hmm, my dear. I wish it was in a good way," he said, driving out of the parking lot. It was still daylight at about 4:30 p.m., and Midowa commented on how he hoped they would not get stuck in too much traffic. In truth he did not care; in fact, he secretly hoped that the car ride would last all night.

"Baby, you must be so hungry. What do you feel like eating? Let's stop somewhere." He put his hand on my lap.

"Eeem, I'm okay o. I just need to shower like asap. I'm sure my aunt will have food in the house."

"Are you sure? Because we can just quickly stop and get takeaway sef. At least then you'll have it in the house just in case."

"Eeem, okay then. I'll take it to go."

"My baby, wow. Welcome to Nigeria." He held my hand. I busied my other hand, like a teenager not used to male company. Lagos life had worn on him a little, and it was intimidating how much of a man he had become.

"It's nice to see your face again. Pictures and video calls are not quite the same," I said, squeezing his hand and trying too hard to be causal. I suddenly panicked, wondering if our connection was gone and would never be the same again.

Midowa parked at a fast-food restaurant, and as we walked in, he pulled me into a side hug. As soon as we walked into the brightly lit restaurant, my stomach started grumbling. I couldn't believe I almost missed the mouth-watering opportunity to experience the most scintillating display of assorted meats and exotic dishes I had ever seen.

"Whoa, is this what you guys call fast food?" I asked.

"Ah, my dear, that's how it is now o. Our own fast food in Naija serves real food."

"No, that's good. I like that. Like they literally have everything here," I said, eyeing a gorgeous stack of cow skin in bright-red tomato stew.

"Everything," Midowa agreed.

I ordered Jollof rice and fried snails, yam porridge, vegetable soup, and *asun,* goat meat porridge. It was way more than I needed, but Midowa coaxed me into trying all the dishes and convinced me that I would be glad I got them. As he paid the bill and asked if I wanted any of the pastries, a TV jingle caught my attention, and I froze in place as the music played. I whipped my head around to look at Midowa. "Chariots of Fire!"

"Ehn?" He leaned in to listen to the melody.

"Chariots of Fire!" I repeated and closed my eyes, letting the memories carry me back to my childhood when the TV station would play that melody at intermission.

"Is that what it's called?" Midowa asked.

I nodded with my eyes still shut. "Gosh, I haven't heard that in forever."

It was already dark by the time we arrived at the house in Adeniran Ogunsanya where I would be staying. The gateman let us in and rushed over to help with our bags. A girl who was about my age ran out to greet us.

"Hi, Tete. Oh my God, look at you!" I hugged my 2nd cousin, who was now much taller than me. Midowa took my suitcase into the house and shook hands with Tete's younger brother.

"Look at you, Samira ehn, Americana. Welcome home o!" Tete said.

I walked into the house and noticed the scent of fried stew as my aunt came out of the kitchen to embrace me.

"Ehh, my daughter is back oo!" I held on to my mum's cousin Aunty Grace, amazed that her voice somehow sounded like Muhmee's. The house bubbled with chatter as my uncle appeared and teased me for being a grownup.

"My dear thank God NEPA decided to give us light o. They must have known you were coming," My uncle commented. I introduced Midowa, and he was invited to stay for dinner. Tete served him and me rice and stew at the dining table while her parents were in the living room. Midowa and I whispered to each other as the cousins periodically wandered in to see if we needed anything. Midowa thanked the family for their hospitality and then left, after giving me a quick hug.

Hours later Midowa texted me saying he hoped I had set up the new SIM card he gave me and wished we had found some time alone before he left.

Yeah, I'm so glad I got that unlocked phone. Thank you so much for the SIM card, I texted back.

Thank God o. I won't have slept if we didn't talk this night. How far have you settled in? he asked.

I took a bath, and now I'm in bed, tired as all heck, I responded.

He called me, and I hesitated for a few minutes before answering. "Hey, baby!" he said enthusiastically.

"Hey, hon," I responded in a whisper. "Sorry, my cousin is asleep, and I don't wanna wake her."

"Ah, sorry. Okay," he whispered in return. "It's so crazy. Now that I've seen you, I miss you more than I did all these years."

"Aww, me too," I responded.

He kept the conversation short and said good night.

⁓ ⁓ ⌁ ⁓ ⁓

I arranged to meet Aunty Silvia at Serendipity Bank for an appointment with her cousin Tolani. I hailed a taxi and eased myself in, feeling like a big girl who would never have to take the bus again in

Nigeria. We came up on some light traffic in a narrow street when I spotted a hawker grilling some corn and *ube*, African pear.

"Oga, please lemme quickly buy corn. Madam, gimme one corn and three pears," I called out to the woman watching the traffic to make sure she was not holding it up. The hawker sprang to her feet, and the exchange of merchandise and money was so smooth that I confirmed that I would always be a Lagos girl. As I nibbled on the snack, I paused and took a picture to send to my parents so they would know what they were missing. I sucked on the creamy inside of the ube, having peeled off the velvety purple skin, grateful that it was still as wonderful as I remembered. Seeing the city of Lagos with fresh eyes, I wondered if I was disappointed because I was now used to better living conditions. Some of my favourite things about Nigeria seemed to have been lost. The mallams no longer sold my beloved chewy candy, goody goody, for one thing, which devastated my inner child.

"Ah, all the companies that used to make those things have packed up oo. Everything is now imported. Just forget this country, abeg," Midowa had explained when I asked him about it. Some of the buildings I remembered as being so magical suddenly appeared ordinary, and the more I ventured out, the more childhood wonders seemed to wither under my critical grown-up eyes.

I arrived at the bank and looked up at the building, gorgeous and looming in pastel pink and cobalt blue. I went into the hall and, finding a spot to sit, called Aunty Silvia, who was running late. About forty-five minutes later, I saw her walk in and be greeted by the clerks. I gathered my handbag and caught up with her while commenting on how fabulous she looked.

"Ah, thank you, my dear. You have to look the part as a businesswoman oo. My business here today is somewhat personal but also official." She flowed as her heels clicked on the floor tiles. We walked into the office of Tolani Bademosi, which was a shared space with three others attending to customers. Aunty Silvia introduced us, and I noticed her job title on a business card: business analyst. The cousins made small talk about family and the fact that Tolani remained unmarried and childless. I got the sense that the woman was not on good terms with her mother, Mrs. Dopesi's aunt.

"Ehn, ehn, you are just lucky o. See how everything is working out for you." Aunty Silvia eyed her cousin enviously and looked around the posh office.

"We thank God oo!" she responded.

I learned that this was one of the better banks, and their structures had gained them favour with the people per aesthetic appeal and staff efficiency. Aunty Tolani told us about her new gig in the bank that had her entertaining some company from America. That was how she got involved in the autism awareness program the bank was working on. She had been lucky enough to be selected amongst the entourage that would flank the group of delegates for the second annual seminar in Lagos.

"It's really a big deal. Our bank is the only one that hosts that kind of program on a large scale." She directed the comment at me, flipping her weave without any intent for modesty.

Mrs. Dopesi gazed thoughtfully at her cousin while she spoke. I caught the looks and surmised from all she had told me that she thought of her cousin as pretentious. On the plane to Lagos, she had filled me on the juicy details of Tolani's life. Apparently, she still thought of her as that small Tola from the history of suffering, a true case of grass to grace. Tola, whose mother worried would never amount to anything even as she cried before her late husband's family for help to pay her tuition. In spite of all the casting and binding the demon of failure from her head, Tola continued to disappoint her mother and eventually dropped out of UNILAG. Fast-forward a few years, and she somehow got a job in the bank and quickly got promoted. Aunty Silvia did not hold back in sharing her suspicion that her cousin, like many others who miraculously slipped into the banking sector in Nigeria, had gotten the job lying on her back. Perhaps after that she did put in a lot of work to climb up to her current position of senior staff. Perhaps she stayed lying on her back with powerful men who made good on their promises.

I took notes whenever Aunty Tolani talked about the program, trying not to be distracted by the juicy backstory of how she came to be associated with foreign dignitaries.

"So, Samira, stay in touch, okay? We'll be sending you updates leading up to the event," she said after a drawn-out banter with her cousin about her funding investment at the bank and the loan that would help her grow her lace fabric business.

"Yes, Aunty, I will. Thank you so much."

When Aunty Silvia had exhausted her interest in her cousin's bragging about corporate clout, she announced that we needed to get going.

"Mummy, well done, ma," the guard at the gate said on our way out.

"Ehen, Benji. How is the family?" Aunty Silvia indulged in the customary niceties given that she knew this particular guard from her frequent visits to the bank.

"We thank God, oh Mummy, Mummy!" For as long as I had lived in the States, I still recognized how his voice dripped with that good old placating politeness to curry favour.

"Have this." I watched as aunty Silvia slipped a one hundred naira note in his palm. He scrunched it up and stuffed it in his pants pocket, acting like nothing happened.

"Mummy, God bless you, ma. Thank you, ma!" He called after her as she waved at him with a dismissive hand. I thanked her for making the time to meet and promised to keep her informed of my success with the program. As I watched her drive off in her Toyota Avalon, I imagined that perhaps she thought God would bless her for such unnecessary acts of charity. Seeing the current state of the country, though, it was in fact necessary for security men such as him who were always worse off financially, save for tips acquired from their corporate acts of begging.

Midowa was picking me up after work to go to his house. I waited for him at a fast-food joint close to the bank in Ikeja.

As the hot breeze blew along the express, it occurred to me that the female Lebanese beggars from my childhood were gone from the streets, as were the many limbless children I used to feel bad for as they pressed up on people in traffic.

"Wait—you know what I haven't been seeing?" My head whipped towards Midowa, syncing memories to reality.

"Where are all those Lebanese women who used to line up on the road begging?" I asked.

"Ah, the government has really tried to remove them from the road." He threw me a meaningful look.

"What of all those ones who were handicapped?"

"Oh, the refugees from Chad. Eem, those ones too have reduced. I haven't really been seeing them." He explained how there came to be that influx of limbless adults and children from a war in Cameroun and other neighbouring countries that people fled.

I stared at him as he reeled off political commentary and realized how well grounded he had become. I imagined he knew the whys, likely from eavesdropping on conversations with his father's company and then rehashing those issues with peers who had likewise garnered some wisdom from their fathers.

I wondered what my life would have been like if I had never left Nigeria. Chances are that I too would have become a knowing member of society. I didn't particularly know such political things about America, other than the main events that were publicly discussed.

I was surprised by the changes I noticed in Lagos—regression and advancement all in one. It seemed that the Nollywood movies I had watched tried to warn me, like the sophisticated flare that I remembered from the past had been lost as people hurriedly chased westernization.

Chapter 13

TWISTED ROOTS

I woke up to the sound of quarrelling coming from the neighbour's compound.

"Thunder fire you dere, you dey crase!" It was still dark, but I had a feeling I had been sleeping for a while.

I dragged my tired body out of bed, experiencing a mix of annoyance and nostalgia. Looking out the window, I saw a woman holding a man by the pants and yelling in his face, not an uncommon scene for the little shantytown on the parallel street from the house. It occurred to me that Americans sounded jovial when angry compared to the cacophony of a raging Nigerian with their God-punish-and-thunder-fire-you invectives. The *f* and *s* bombs in between Western *r*'s and soft *th*'s were child's play compared to the sting of the gravity-defying African curse.

It was just 4:30 a.m., but people were already walking the streets, going about their day. I picked up my phone and turned off the alarm, which would have sounded at five. Cousin Tete was going with me to visit Grandma Ufi in Kano. I had about an hour and a half before we had to be at the commercial bus park. I opened my suitcase to make sure it was fully packed so that I would not forget the things Muhmee got for her.

Hours later, we boarded a comfortable coaster bus packed with people of all sorts heading to the north.

"Ha, you want to go by road? Why don't you people just fly?" Muhmee had asked me over the phone.

"Hmm, Muhmee to come and enter plane again? Abeg, lemme stay on the ground. Meanwhile, Tete dem said it will be fun to see the scenery," I had told her. Midowa too had expressed concerns about my safety on the road, but I convinced him that it was fine since my cousin would be with me and we were going in the daytime.

Cousin Tete pointed out monuments as we drove through dirt red and thick forested roads and into the densely populated cities. As expected, we came upon traffic in every major city, and I prayed we would not end up travelling late into the night. Cousin Tete made sure to buy me everything that hawkers shoved in our faces as soon as the bus slowed down. We got out at rest stops to stretch our legs and, regrettably, to use the bathrooms from my worst nightmare.

Grandma Ufi received us at the bus park when we arrived in Kano after eleven hours of travelling.

I hugged and looked up at the stately woman in a long flowing bubu dress and a matching head tie. She looked familiar from my childhood memories and pictures, but I had already decided that she was a stranger. To me, she was the notorious woman who wanted only a long-distance relationship with her family, it seemed. I did not know what to expect on the visit but knew it was worth the satisfaction that Muhmee was getting out of it.

"Mira, Mira, see how big you are now." She beamed at me on the car ride to her house. Cousin Tete and I were in the back seat while she barked instructions at the driver.

"Yes, ma." I smiled sheepishly, praying that I would not be caught being disrespectful.

We got to the house, and I saw people filtering in and out like it was a hotel and not a residence. Grandma Ufi greeted nearly everyone she saw as she motioned us inside the duplex.

"My dear, please come. This is your room. Just relax, ehn. They will bring water for you to bathe. Fatima kawo mata ruwa."

I picked up a familiar word, *Meruwa*, and turned to Tete as Grandma walked out.

"Is Meruwa not the people who carry the tins of water on their shoulders?"

"That's them. You still remember. Do you know any other Hausa words?"

"Only the ones Muhmee says when she abuses people."

"I trust my aunty," she snickered.

I put down my bags and looked around the dimly lit room. Grandma Ufi had a house help who kept some order in the residence by the look of things. I smiled to myself, thinking how different Muhmee's life would be if she were as spoiled as her mother. I wondered if the woman ever missed the maternal feeling of having a child of her own in the house. If she did, she certainly didn't show it. The house was a three-bedroom duplex, much too big for a single woman with no children but sufficiently teeming with company. I peeled off my clothes from the long sweaty journey, happy that the ventilation was good. I was also pleased that the power was staying on so far, and my sanity did not have to compete with the roaring of overworked generators.

The house help, Fatima, had fetched me water and put out soap and a towel with bathroom slippers.

I could not believe I had braved the journey to Kano, a place I had visited only as a small child. I liked the crisp air of the city, noting that it felt and smelled lighter than Lagos. That night, the power went off as I was about to fall asleep. I hissed in frustration and hoped that it would come back before the heat and mosquitoes descended on me. I felt a strong wind rush into the room, carrying a familiar smell that stirred something in me. I got up and walked to the window, where I heard voices in the distance and surprisingly felt grounded. A few minutes later, the rain came down heavily, and I inhaled the sweet scent of clay earth in the neighbourhood. I stood there for a long time, feeling one with nature while childhood memories flooded me, the joyful and the melancholy. I realized that having constant power in the States had distracted me from tranquil moments like this.

The next morning Grandma Ufi greeted me with a song apparently from my childhood. She exuded so much joy, I wondered if she was putting it on for me or if she had in fact cracked the code to life. We ate the traditional breakfast of sweet bread and kunu. She excitedly reminded me of things that I had enjoyed as a child and how I needed to try them again.

She insisted I call her Kaka even though Tete called her Okwo, Grandma in Igala. She was sister to Tete's grandmother, who still maintained her identity to Kogi state.

Cousin Tete went out later to do some shopping. I wanted to go with her but period cramps held me back. She said she preferred it that way, fearing that something would happen to me.

I lounged with Grandma Ufi in the living room, chewing on tiger nuts and relishing the familiar creaminess.

"Kaka, what about my grandfather? Do you still see him?" I asked.

"Eeemm, sometimes, but he doesn't greet me oo, so me, I just go my own way," she said, her voice dropping to a childlike tone. I was impressed that inspite of her basic secondary school education, she spoke quite eloquently.

I wondered, as I had done so many times, how Aunty Zubaida felt about not having a relationship with her father. Muhmee seemed to have made her peace with it and did not resent her mother, but I thought it was particularly unfair to Aunty Zubaida to have been robbed of that security.

"I wish we could visit him," I said, knowing even as the words left my mouth that it was a lost cause. "How did you two even meet?"

"Hmm, Samira, Samira. You are just like your name, ehn?"

"Ehen, please, what does my name actually mean because Muhmee tells me different things?" I asked, glad that the opportunity finally came up.

"Somebody who is lively, that like to gist." She leaned over and pinched my cheek.

Grandma Ufi quickly changed the subject. "Ehen, so, my dear, how long will you be staying in Lagos again?"

"Till December, after my program. I'll stay for some weeks"

"Ehn, ehn, ok that's good o. This your program is very important to bring you all the way from America, abi is there someone that you came to visit?" She winked as she threw some nuts in her mouth.

I laughed. "Ah, I came to visit you, nau, Kaka." I winked back.

"Hmm, see, my dear, our people say that what a child will see from the top of a tree, an old person will see sitting down. I have seen it all, gaskiya faa."

I wanted to indulge her and talk about Midowa, but I suddenly felt that it was hard to say his name. Something about the rain had turned my thoughts deep into the abyss and I could no longer recall the feelings I'd had before.

"There's somebody I've known for a long time, but I'm not sure."

"Ehen! My daughter, tell me about him then." The excitement in her eyes caused her wrinkle lines to almost disappear. I started from the beginning and told her every detail that I could remember. I told her parts of the story that I had never shared with anyone, not my mother, not Aunty Zubaida, not even Nayana. Grandma Ufi interrupted me at times to ask questions that would make me delve deeper into the account, hands flying everywhere. It struck me how similar my mannerisms were to my grandma's.

"Cheyaa faa, so is he coming to meet you in the US? I hope you're not coming back for him o." It tickled me the slight high pitch in her voice when she advised me, just like Muhmee.

"No, I don't think so." I heard my response and was surprised by how certainly I had answered that. I had imagined Grandma Ufi as a careless romantic because of the way she kept chasing her Alhaji. I found it surprising that she was not prompting me to follow my heart and come home for a boy.

Tete returned from the market, cutting the conversation short. Grandma Ufi whispered to me, "We will continue the gist tomorrow." I chuckled and met her eyes. It seemed that this childlike nature was the secret to her youthful vitality.

We examined Tete's goody bag as items came out, some for me and some for her siblings. She handed me a bunch of waist beads, saying how much she thought I would like them.

She was right. I hurried into the bedroom to see how they looked, shimmering on my wide hips.

"Hmm, the guy is in trouble ooo," Grandma teased when I showed her. To which I shook my head, hoping that Tete would not catch on.

I spent the rest of the day telling stories about life in America and how different things were. I injected stories about Aunty Zubaida and how she had independently made her way into the workforce and was doing her thing.

Grandma Ufi took it all in, smiling and clapping her hands dramatically as she exclaimed, "That's my daughter!"

After dinner we said good night, and I lingered in the living room, hoping to sneak onto the balcony when everyone was gone. I was so happy she had one; balconies often gave me an opportunity to process things. I missed mine back home.

I stepped out to the familiar scent of harmattan setting in. There were trees lined up the side of the house, covering a significant amount of land. I inhaled deeply thinking how different the air was from Lagos. In the darkness there were spots of light coming from homes spread farther apart than in the congested Lagos. I looked up at the sky and counted five stars. It occurred to me that I had not seen stars in a while. The tree branches shivered like they had been roused. I leaned in closer, hugging my arms as they rested on the rails. It felt like a good seventy-five degrees Fahrenheit; I couldn't think what it would be in Celsius.

The breeze gushed slowly at first, rustling the leaves. I listened to the sound of the trees while attempting to quiet my mind. Nayana's words swirled in my brain: *You either claim him or cut him loose.* I quivered as I heard a heavy breeze rush towards me and raised my face to the sensation of being caressed by the wind. It was a deep, almost tangible sensation that felt like hands. I moved my face around, as if feeling the wind with it. The breeze softened and started to withdraw. With my eyes still shut, I directed my attention slowly from my face down through my body. My breathing exercises with the kids were going to come in handy. I frowned as my inside eyes examined my organs to get in touch with every happening in there. The beating of my heart seemed fast, a certain flutter that was telling me something. My chest was pounding hard; blood was being pumped to keep up with some madness that was disrupting my well-being.

"*I wish I could meet my grandfather,*" I caught myself thinking, not sure if those were even true thoughts.

My arms tingled. The wind smoothed back my arm hair as it raged and roared. Goose bumps popped up on my skin and I silently pleaded for the wind to withdraw its force, to return to being gentle to me. I decided it was time to get back inside as I was feeling cold. I opened my eyes and stood up straight. The wind retreated, and the tree branches, equally disappointed to end their dance, shivered to a standstill. They seemed to know my heart was troubled.

The trees were not capricious like me; they swayed only in the face of eruptive wind. But when they stood still, they were sure in their stillness. I wanted more than anything to be like that. To be able to be still and only move when I have to. But then there were trees that bent easily in the wind and that were then harder to break. I thought of Aunty Zubaida as such a tree, elastic and able to bounce back.

The distant chatter in Hausa filled me with nostalgia, and I missed my mum. It was nice to hear the language with which she taught me life's moral lessons. I could almost hear her saying,

"Kaman mahaukaci yana gudu daga wanan bishiya zuwa wani bishiya." Basically, I was behaving like a madman running from tree to tree.

She often said that when I couldn't stick to one thing. I heard that expression throughout my childhood until one day, she finally explained what it meant.

There was a mad man where Muhmee grew up in Kano, who was known to dance half -naked in the market to a song that only he could hear. Some people would throw money at him, grateful for the free entertainment but quietly saddened that soldiers would soon be along to whip him as they did any disrupters in public places. The madman would occasionally pause mid-dance and take off in a sprint, yelling, "Don't beat me o," hiding under the nearest tree he could find. He would then run from tree to tree, dancing at intervals before continuing his sprint. It became a point of reference in the neighbourhood that a person who could not make up their mind was called the madman running between trees.

I asked Grandma Ufi the next day if this story were true.

"Your mummy liked that story, ehn." She laughed. "Ah I remember when he died. Oh, everybody was sad. *Gaskiya*, he didn't disturb anybody."

"How did he die?" I asked.

"Motor jammed him.," She sighed. "And the man was a good dancer, ehn?" She kept her eyes fixed on the yam she was cutting. I studied her face when she was not looking, trying to guess her age, as it was never told to me. I decided by math that she was about 70 and even then there were only few wrinkles on her face. Her hands had more lines, a thing she attributed to overuse of hot water to skin chicken. She had a breezy way about her, like she bore no grudges. That would have been easy for her, as she dodged responsibilities. No additional stressors to age her.

After a long paused, I chuckled and said, "so the man used to hide under the tree so that they wouldn't catch him?"

"Ehhm, one time the soldiers were shooting up and the bullet killed one man standing there, so maybe he was hiding so that the bullet will not kill him, ehen."

"Ah, okay." I nodded, fascinated that in this man's quest for safety he became a satire for indecisiveness. And yet although people judged his actions to be foolish, he actually was doing what any sane person would do when threatened. *Move away from danger and find cover.* He was acting on the premise of personal safety, a base need according to Maslow's hierarchy. As people looked on at a madman displaying his madness, I pictured a person striving for self-actualization, whatever that meant for him. I found the madman's story sad but also validating. Sometimes our actions or inactions might not make sense to others but in fact demonstrate our own shrewdness, however flawed. Maybe Grandma Ufi was also like that madman, running away from impending danger in what would appear to be an irresponsible way.

I watched her youthful face as she worked away at the yam, slicing with precision. What did she make of her life now? Was it worth it for her to have pursued a married man at the expense of a committed life of self-respect? Granted, she was doing well financially, with a successful textile business and the community in her corner. Maybe she had it all and wouldn't undo any of her past as a reckless romantic.

The next morning at the bus park, I promised her that I would keep in touch and chat with her on WhatsApp.

"Kaka, make sure you check your phone," I implored her with one last hug.

"I will, my daughter. Please take care o. Bye." Her smile was genuine and almost mournful. Like she was saying goodbye for the last time. I felt my eyes welling and almost wanted to get off the bus to stay with her. I concluded that she did want family; she did need family.

By the time we returned to Lagos, I missed my grandma so much, it felt almost like I had left another home. I had enjoyed the visit much more than I imagined. I got to see her stores and met some of her closest friends who cherished her like a blood relative. People loved the woman, and I could see why. I just couldn't reconcile her emotional detachment from her daughter. In any case, I decided that like my mother, I would love the good nature in the woman and forgive the failings.

Midowa picked me up the next day to select my screening materials for the seminar. The event was to be held in a conference hall in the Ikeja part of Lagos. I opted for the hot breeze against the AC and really got a chance to see how the streets were filled with people who are labelled mad, with ragged clothes and matted hair that sometimes had remnants of food from the dump site they slept in.

We stopped at his house to say hello to his parents. I greeted his mother, to which she responded, "Ehen, my dear wow you've changed o. How are you? How are your parents?"

I thought she had that same tired tone I was finding characteristic of the women I used to respect. They all seemed different. Beyond getting older, I sensed a quiet animosity that they held towards me, a sort of resentment in their attempts to show that life had not left them behind. I shuddered to think that this could have been my reunion with Aunty Zubaida if she had not come with us. When I left Nigeria, I relished the idea that my status would be elevated above my peers and that when I came back to visit, I would floor them with my new accent and American aura. I had no idea how alienating that move would turn out to be for relationships. I had loosely kept in touch with some people, doing the best I could in the incredibly fast-paced life of America. Truly, how many people can one keep in touch with at the same time?

"Ah, is this my Tega?" I saw that he had become a nineteen-year-old who was fifty-two kilograms of pure testosterone. He still played football with the big boys on the street, all shirtless and rascally. He mostly ignored me but was interested in whatever gifts I brought him.

"I still have that necklace o," I called after him as he bounced out of the living room, eating one of the chocolate bars I got him.

"Are you serious?" Midowa looked pleased. "That's a good sign," he whispered, almost inaudibly.

After catching up with the family, it occurred to me that the sweet spot of moving to America was somewhere between the idea of returning and the actual return. If I had visited home every year, that would have helped me keep up with the changes that the people I knew were going through and they in turn with mine. Maybe then they would have seen that I was still the same person, except that like everybody else, I changed as a result of being older. Of course this change was happening to me in the American context, which undeniably influenced me. But people assumed I was just acting brand new. I couldn't really explain to them the hard adjustments that I was forced to make in the US while still not quite fitting in or how hard it is to find African spices to make food or how flimsy conversations about hair and skin colour become the defining story of one's life. No, these people couldn't contemplate my own struggles, nor could my American friends. In the end it felt like I had traded a familiar world for the image of another. There was no dream to find; the dream was only in the process of dreaming. That was the sweet spot.

Chapter 14

A NEXUS OF CARING

It was now about a week before the seminar and I woke up that morning to get ready for some sightseeing with Midowa. By this point, I felt like I was slowly getting over the jet lag and returning to a good sleeping pattern. As I pulled on my jeans, I heard someone whistling noisily in the backyard and looked out the window. Sure enough it was Uncle Festus, the house driver.

Uncle Festus was a character. He would be whistling so early in the morning that it became synonymous with the sound of the early morning prayers at the mosques. I typically woke up to the morning heat, the sound of people going about their business, and the kids stomping their little feet to school. Uncle Festus lived in the boys' quarters at the back of the main house. In the evenings he would linger by the kitchen door, teasing the house help about this and that and then praise her according to the height of his dinner plate.

When he washed the car in the morning, he would whistle and sing loudly and deliberately, almost as if to invite conversation. I walked out to the balcony to greet him.

"Good morning, Uncle Festus!" I found myself downplaying my American accent when I talked to him.

"Good morning, my dear. It's a good day to be alive, huhn." He, on the contrary, took on a more nasal tone and inserted an *r* sound into every word. I hoped he would launch into one of his sermons about politicians and their betrayals. He would yell random expressions of frustration about the state of the country. It was highly entertaining, and I appreciated his sharp insights. Spending time with Midowa, I developed an appetite for current events in the country and tucked away every nugget I heard to process with him later.

Uncle Festus started singing a gospel song as he circled the car to wash the tires. I watched him carefully scrape the scum from the farthest part of the wheels.

"Come and fetch me water, boy," he called out to the neighbour's son, who looked like he had been trying his best to stay out of sight. "Use that jerrican," he added. It tickled me to hear him say *jerrican*, as it flooded me with nostalgia. As the boy dragged his feet to the tap in front of the house, Uncle Festus went on a tangent about how some of the politicians are like Australian bushmen. It would be a better thing if we had as president a man of his calibre who carries himself with dignity. Meanwhile, I was sure that I had seen him stumbling around drunk when I came home one night.

"They will steal all that money and go scot-free!" He continued talking to no one in particular. I got the sense that he was speaking for my benefit. Especially at times when he would talk about how the state of affairs was chasing people away from the country so much so that Nigerian children are now being raised without a cultural foundation.

The boy returned with a small plastic container filled with water. Uncle Festus took the jug out of his hand and, after examining it, shoved it dramatically to the boy's chest.

"My friend, is this water going to be enough for me to wash this big car? Come on, will you go get me a big jerrican, you nincompoop," he added with comedic exaggeration. I almost burst out laughing and bit my lip. Shaking my head, I decided to go back inside to finish getting ready and caught him smiling at his own antics. I felt sure that when I left, Uncle Festus would mourn the loss of a very keen audience.

Midowa picked me around 10 a.m. to beat the traffic going from the mainland to the island. I was concerned that he was missing work that day, but he assured me that it was fine.

We went to the National Museum to, according to Midowa, ground me in Nigerian history.

The sombre tone of the display room and the drone of the guide's voice left me with such an eerie feeling that I pulled closer to Midowa and grabbed his arm. He adjusted his glasses and smirked, whispering information about artefacts and historical figures on display. Whenever he got stuck, he deferred to the guide, who proceeded to drop flirtatious compliments about my outfit. I asked how Midowa knew so much and he reminded me that our class had toured the museum back in our school days but I didn't get to go. He said that he kept looking out for me that day, disappointed that I didn't come. He had only half listened and spent the whole time plotting a strategy to have a conversation with me back at school.

We approached the infamous black car that former president Murtala Muhammed was assassinated in. Sitting in the middle of the lobby, it appeared well maintained save for the fact that it was riddled with bullets, and the insides were covered in shards of glass. I grasped Midowa's hand and looked away, only to be confronted with the faces of past politicians scowling over the scene. I suddenly wanted to leave and hurried Midowa to look at the figurines outside.

When we left the premises, Midowa noticed I was quiet.

"Hey, are you okay?" he asked.

"Yeah," I huffed. "Man, I remember hearing about the president when we were growing up, but seeing that car was too much for me. I think I saw dried blood in there." I grimaced.

"Heya, sorry, babe. You know here we're used to that type of thing."

"How?"

"Ah, do you know how many times I've seen cars after robbers attack or even police sef? I'm used to it." He shrugged and started the car.

"Hmm, I don't remember things being that crazy in Nigeria," I mumbled.

"You've been gone for a while now, so you won't know. It's even the police who are the main problem for us, especially young guys like me."

"That's crazy . . ." My voice trailed off, and Midowa grabbed my hand.

"Fear, fear! Please don't be scared. We own these streets notin dey happen. Lagos is mad fun, especially at night," he said squeezing my hand. "So do you still want to see a movie?"

"Eeem, it will be late, nau. Let's plan for another day."

"Hmm, okay. The only problem is now it's already five thirty, so there'll be traffic leaving the island. You know what? Let's just hang out at the mall for some time to let the traffic die down and then we can head out."

"Okay, if you think that's best."

"Yeah, because if not, it's to just be burning fuel. Do you want something to eat?" he asked as we came upon light traffic leaving Onikan.

Bon Jovi's "You Give Love a Bad Name" came on the radio just then. He turned it up and bobbed his head.

"Buy gala!" He looked in the direction of the street hawker. He sucked his lips loudly to get her attention. It was a small girl of about ten years old with a very mournful look on her face.

"Shey you'll eat?" he asked me.

"Sure, I haven't eaten gala since I came o,"

"Ehhn what have you been doing with your life?"

"Eating other things," I responded.

Still grooving to the music, he moulded his hand in the shape of a microphone and shoved it an inch away from my mouth.

I stuttered, trying to remember the lyrics to the song.

"Ahnahn, you don't know this song?" he asked me.

"I can't remember o. I don't really listen to songs like this in the US."

His microphone hand dropped with obvious disappointment.

"Ehn, ehn, so what do you listen to?"

"I'm really into jazz now and house music."

"Hmm, American girl." He put his window down as the gala girl approached.

"Gimme two gala," he called to her.

He got change from the girl and said, "Ehen, omo dada. Good girl."

He waved goodbye to her as she curtsied repeatedly. It looked like he had let her keep some of the change, as the most grateful smile appeared on her innocent, pain-stoned face.

He handed me one, and I glanced at him as he opened his. His jaw seemed a little tense, and I couldn't help thinking it was the whole music thing. Midowa had put me on to his taste in music, and I caught on like an obedient protégé. He used to find so much satisfaction in that. So many years had passed, I wondered if he expected that I would stay frozen in the time we had spent together.

We toured the mall, and I was amazed that it was comparable to the malls in America. The stores were just as glitzy with overpriced merchandise. My stomach growled as we approached the food court, and Midowa insisted that we go into a joint called Nando's. They had the best barbecue chicken I had eaten in a while, and I took some burgers and fries to go. As we walked out and admired the stores from a distance, my eyes fell on a woman with a little girl whom I presumed was her daughter. Midowa called to the woman to get her attention, and without warning he pulled me by the hand towards her.

"Ah, good evening, ma." He bowed as he greeted her. I also said a greeting and turned my eyes to the little girl, who looked about five. Midowa picked up the young girl, pinching her cheeks as he talked to her mother. She was a sweet little thing, and as I watched Midowa's face, it occurred to me that he loved kids and kids loved him. Everywhere we went, it was like kids suddenly appeared so that they could be near him.

"Ma, this is my friend Samira. She is visiting from America to run a program about disabilities in children."

I stared at him, trying to decipher that introduction, when I noticed that he was throwing me all kinds of signals with his eyes.

"Yes, ma. It's a seminar about recognizing autism and helping parents to manage it." Out of the corner of my eye, I caught Midowa breathe a sigh of relief that I had decoded the look.

"Sorry, what did you call it?" the woman asked.

"Sorry, ma. Let me see if I have a flyer in my bag." I reached in and pulled out one that had been wrinkled from being in there for too long.

"Here you go, ma. Please come. You'll learn so much, and it will help anybody you know." I looked down at the little girl, who was now back at her mother's side, searching for signs of any neurodiverse behaviour.

"Ehn, ehn, okay. I will look at it. Thanks, dear." She scanned the paper, visibly confused but interested.

"How is your son? What's his name again?" Midowa asked her.

"Doyin. He's fine, dear. How are your parents?" she responded.

"They're fine, ma." As I listened to the conversation, it finally dawned on me who she was.

Midowa concluded with pleasantries and said goodbye to the little girl, who waved frantically.

"Is that the woman with the son?" I asked him, grabbing his arm as we walked away.

"Yeah baby. My neighbour," he responded.

"Heya, that's her daughter too?"

"Yeah. She's younger than him. She seems normal, very playful."

"Heya, I really hope she comes then. Please, if you see her again, remind her," I said, wishing I had met her earlier now that it was only a week before the event.

It was 7:30 p.m and traffic was surprisingly lighter than usual. Midowa was right; he really knew the city like the back of his hand. He could always predict where the traffic would be, and he knew ways to dodge it.

We were coming up to a narrow bend to make the turn into Oshodi express, a straight shot to home, according to Midowa.

"Did Nayana say anything about what she thought of Lagos?" I asked Midowa as we talked about everything and nothing on the stretch of road.

"Ehn, she said some nice things sha. I think she was afraid to complain to me. She was very happy about the animals she took pictures of, especially the lizards. All these American people." He chuckled. "You know how they are. She said they greet her by the window in the morning."

I laughed, shaking my head.

"Then she told me her dog's name is Mango," he continued. "I was like, ahnahn, you named your dog mango?" I imagined how his tone would have been rich with ridicule, every word stressed in true Nigerian sarcasm.

"Yeah, because he's cute like a mango!" Midowa blurted out in his best impression of an American accent.

"And he's a cairn terrier." I pinched my nose, and we both laughed.

Midowa shook his head and said, "American princess." He shifted in his seat and slowed down behind a truck in front of us. We were approaching a spot on a narrow bridge, and the truck seemed to be lagging just ahead.

"Please leave my friend, jor." I shoved him. "I also have a cat named Rus—" I was cut off by a loud bang on the car door. It sounded like it came from the back end of Midowa's side, like the tire had exploded. Startled, I put my hands between my legs, hoping that Midowa wouldn't notice they were shaking. I looked over at Midowa. His temple seemed to be beating at the same pace as my heart was pounding out of my chest. Next thing I knew, a man suddenly appeared outside Midowa's door with a black shape in his hand.

My heart jumped into my throat when a coarse voice ordered us not to move. I gripped the door handle to settle my shaking nerves. My stomach revolted, and I dreaded the thought of soiling myself and possibly Midowa's car.

"Money, phone Now! Now!" The man screamed in a scratchy voice that scraped at my chest and made my heart beat faster. Something told me that he was putting on that gruffness to mask his identity. That didn't make me any less terrified. I kept my eyes on Midowa, praying that the man wouldn't shoot him in the head. He didn't look as panicked as I was, and I tried to mirror his calm.

I reached down for my bag, fumbling for what, I wasn't even sure. I debated whether to hand the thief my whole bag or just hold out my phone. Midowa's eyes seemed to dance around his head, and I hoped that he was hatching an escape plan.

"Guy, take. Take we'll give you. Hold on! Hold on!" Midowa threw his phone out the window. I took his cue and was about to pull mine out when the car suddenly screeched off. As my heart slowly settled back into my chest, I realized that we had somehow managed to get past the truck, and there was no traffic in front of us. Bewildered, I looked back and saw that Midowa had miraculously maneuvered a narrow space between the truck and the barricade.

"Thank God," I whispered, panting. I looked over at Midowa, and his face was so tight I could see a throbbing vein on his head. His breathing was heaving and forced, like fumes were coming out of his nose. He didn't respond but just kept driving, his foot a little heavy on the pedal.

"Bastards," he finally spoke, almost in a foreign whisper. I opened my mouth but then shut it again, hoping that the road would be clear. I was certain that any more traffic would cause him to erupt.

I willed my breathing to slow as it dawned on me that I had forgotten about Midowa's temper in our school days. I wanted to get home, take a bath, and crawl into bed and not tell anyone what had happened.

When I went to sleep that night, my chest was still pounding as I thought about how far I had moved on from life in Lagos, which had once been familiar to me but now was so foreign.

⁓ ⁓ ⌐ ⌐ ⁓

The day of the event arrived. It was a Friday, and Midowa risked incurring his uncle's wrath by taking another day off. He picked me up at 6:30 a.m. to make it to the island for the program's scheduled start time of 8:00 a.m. The robbery incident was now a week behind us and while I shuddered to think that it would have ended badly, Midowa made light of it.

As the cool morning breeze blew along the express, he quizzed me about the assignments I had been given and asked for the thousandth time how he could help. I explained that I would be shadowing one of the therapists as they worked and observing the clients to see how they presented. I was to follow along with a diagnosis checklist, and at the end of the day, we would compare notes and see how many come up positive for autism spectrum disorder.

"Ehen, you said they're coming shey?" I asked him.

"Yup, that's what she said. She will bring her son," he replied, referring to his neighbour.

"Okay, cool."

When we reached the arena, Midowa parked the car, breathing a sigh of relief that he had delivered me there on time. I adjusted my grey blazer, dusted my black quarter-length pants, and made sure my white T-shirt was still spotless. As he got out of the car, Midowa got a call from a co-worker who was wondering why he was not in for the day. I heard him explain to the person that he was at a seminar for autism awareness. I smiled as he eloquently described the day's events and asked the co-worker to stop by if he could. I was so proud to hear him explain autism in words that he had heard from me, words that were very different from the ones he had been using in the past. We walked to the entrance, and I spotted my mentor from

America, Ms. Sophia Taylor, to whom I was assigned. We had met on collection day, and she showed me the assessment tools we would be using for consultation. I dismissed Midowa with a quick hug and asked him to find a seat.

I greeted Aunty Tolani, and she introduced me to the organizers.

"Wow, Aunty. You look lovely." I complimented her dress, noting how comfortably she mingled with intellectuals. Too bad Aunty Silvia would not be coming to see it for herself. I was watching people move around the lobby when my eyes caught sight of a tall woman with short hair. I looked away, and when I glanced back, the woman had turned around. I recognized her!

When she spoke, I felt nostalgia immediately wash over me. I walked up to her, concerned that she might not remember me but desperate to make a connection.

I touched her shoulder lightly, and as the woman turned around, I said, "Excuse me, Osaruwa Gospel?" I remembered the first time Osaruwa joined our class in SS1. She was a big-boned nineteen-year-old whose hand was tightly grasped by her mother as she scanned the faces of the students in her daughter's new class. I remembered the way Mrs. Gospel's eyes had fallen on mine. It was a fleeting moment, but I had caught a silent plea in her eyes as she entrusted her daughter to the care of strangers, hoping that they had been trained from their homes to be decent.

"Yes?" the woman responded, her head cocked to the side as she leaned in with her right eye. Her face registered recognition, and she smiled, flashing the familiar sparkling gap teeth.

"It's me, Samira, from Mrs. Ukene's SS1 class."

"Samira! Y-y-yes, I rem-m-m-member you!" I detected a bit of an accent, punctuated by the significant stutter that I knew so well. Osaruwa was now even taller than the five foot ten she was as a teen, carrying her impressive build with an uneven stance. Her thick jet-black hair was in a supreme Afro, which I found out back in school was a permanent look because her injured scalp could not withstand hair braiding.

Osaruwa had been in an accident at the age of four that left her with a traumatic brain injury and a paralyzed left side. She grew up with one good eye and limited vision in the other, causing her to squint and hold items inches from her nose. Looking at her now, she had on bright-red lipstick, and I remembered that back in school, her lips always had a reddish tint from the cherry lip gloss that she was obsessed with.

We hugged each other. I held her tightly, as if we had been close. We were not. In fact, I felt my face get hot and my vision start to blur as I thought how unfortunate it was that I had not developed a friendship with Osaruwa in school. I had been nice to her at times, helping her look for things or removing obstacles from her path. Yet I realized that even though I knew to defend Osaruwa when our classmates talked about how annoying they found her, I had not. Even though I wanted to stand up to the notorious students who would mock her paralyzed walk or the confused look of her face that caused her eyes to cross, I had not.

Not like Ezioma.

Ezioma was appointed as a sort of guardian for Osaruwa in our class through teachers' recommendations. She shared a seat with Osaruwa, and they always seemed to be having comical conversations. Ezioma was the one who told me about the cherry lip gloss obsession, and even though it left me curious, I and the greater part of our class never cared to get to know the girl. The only time we really paid attention to Osaruwa was when we would queue up to feel the scars underneath the thicket of her gorgeous curls. Osaruwa seemed to enjoy the rare moment of attention and chuckled the whole time as some of us remarked how we wished our hair was like hers. Osaruwa was the oldest student in our class and would ordinarily have been deferred to as the class captain for that reason but also for having the stature of one who could render a halting blow to any of the boys. But instead Osaruwa would sit by herself while students circled her like they were taking turns petting a new puppy, only to then disengage and carry on with their affairs.

"What are you doing here?" I asked her.

"I'm presenting with our company, Capable Hands," she stuttered.

"Wow. That's so cool. How is your mum?"

I remembered Osaruwa's mum with slight regret. I hoped that the woman did not still think of me as a terrible person. Mrs. Gospel had informed the class that due to Osaruwa's brain injury, she got confused easily and forgot things, something that Ezioma would covetously explain to others, with her neck hanging like a doctor explaining a diagnosis. Osaruwa's pens and books were labelled with her name, and yet there were incidents when she would accuse classmates of taking her things. One day she went to our class teacher, Mrs. Ukene, to report that I had taken her pen. I had tried to patiently assure her that the pen was not hers, reminding her that she had hers labelled. I had watched Osaruwa pull the pen up to her right eye, turning it around with a confused look that betrayed any certainty she had when she decided to accuse me of stealing. I had thrown an impatient look at the class teacher, who tapped her chest with her hand, signalling for me to remain calm. In the end it was recommended that I apologize to Osaruwa and let her keep the pen. I did that but decided to keep my distance from Osaruwa to avoid any more accusations. After that incident I felt that Mrs. Gospel was always throwing suspicious looks at me when she would pick her daughter up after school.

"She's fine. She's at home," Osaruwa responded.

"Heya, please greet her for me."

We heard the emcee announce that the program was starting and agreed to meet up again during the break to catch up on each other's lives.

A classy looking woman was the first speaker. She gave an overview of her experiences travelling across the country. I sat in the second row with my mentor, keeping my eyes on the stage and feeling quite relevant. Midowa was seated a distance behind me, and I could feel his gaze on my back.

The speaker went on. "How is this supposed to work? We can have all the programs in the world and all the experts in the world come to help us, but the change needs to start from inside. Because of a prolonged history of bitterness towards the government, Nigerians are now quick to blame everything on them. The government didn't ask us to lock up our handicapped and mentally ill loved ones. Granted, if there were resources established with proper funding and maintenance, that would have been the practice of only a few. Still, the problem stems from a cultural misunderstanding of the foundation, the root cause of these issues. We have some resources, but on a personal level, there is a fear of using them, the stigma of which runs deep."

My phone vibrated, and I took it out to see a message from Midowa.

Serious student. I can see you as you're stretching your neck.

Before nko, you never know if I'll get hired today, I typed discreetly, hoping that my mentor wouldn't judge me.

I would hire you looking like that.

I'm sorry, was that a compliment?

You're breathtaking. That's a compliment. I don't know how someone can be getting finer every day.

I pursed my lips and felt my mentor's eyes hovering over my phone. I quickly flipped to my browser page and pretended to be reading something important.

You're cute, Midowa texted again, and I put the phone away, feeling slightly uncomfortable.

"The change has to start from within." I refocused on the speaker, and those words sank deep into my brain. I wished I could go back to my childhood and change all those reactions that I had displayed towards people with disabilities and unexplained mental illness. "If the little child in school was taught from home to be sympathetic towards anyone who looks or acts differently, how much would that alleviate the bullying, rejection, and isolation that disabled kids have to face at school, for a start, and then in the larger community? This is why awareness is so important, for our children, for your sons, nephews, and nieces, and for my daughter."

During Osaruwa's segment, she promoted the work that her company does in schools for children with physical and learning disabilities.

At the intermission, I was consumed with my checklist when I heard Midowa's voice. I took him over to Osaruwa and introduced them. He vaguely remembered her, but she didn't recognize him. Osaruwa told us that after secondary school, her aunt had taken her to the US, where she went through therapy and then to Boston University. I heard the maturity in her voice and wished our classmates could see her now. Her colleague Erica was also from the US and talked about their behaviour analysis programs with kids in special education.

"Do you guys ever use restraints?" I couldn't wait to ask her.

"You know, that's a tough one. We just started using a new de-escalation model to see if we can eliminate restraints, so we're working on it. At least we're down the usual number we get, so hopefully we'll see some results."

"That's interesting. I'm very curious to see what the alternatives are because that thing is a killer." I caught sight of a young man weaving through the crowd with a massive set of headphones over his ears. As he bounced along, his head bobbed so enthusiastically that I wondered what he was listening to.

Mr. Hip-Hop, I dubbed him, concluding that just like his peers of this generation, he was brainwashed by the hip-hop mentality. *Ndi ala*—mad people, as my dad would say.

"For you or the kids?" Erica snickered.

"Everyone," I responded, hoping I wasn't making a bad impression.

"Yeah, it's tough. I mean, you figure it's really supposed to be a last resort, right, but sometimes it seems like the first thing we wanna do."

"Right. I mean, what do you do when a kid is trying to harm someone else or themselves?"

"True. I don't know. I'd like to think we need to do better at using our therapeutic interventions so that things don't even escalate to that point." She took a sip from her can of Coke.

"I imagine there's some kind of research that's going into that."

"Oh yeah. We have a group of graduate students working on it."

"I'd love to hear what they find. I think we need to implement that at my place too."

"Mm-hmm, sure. Here's my card. Let's keep in touch," she said, coming up from her drink.

"Great. Thank you so much!" I tucked the card into my wallet.

Mr. Hip-Hop walked towards us, and as he got closer, I noticed he was mouthing the lyrics of whatever he was listening to in a very exaggerated manner. He approached us, and Erica greeted him.

"Hey, Tai!" She patted him on the back and introduced him to us.

"Hello," the young man responded in a deep voice that sounded almost mechanical. I wondered why he didn't take off his head-phones to talk to us and noticed that his mouth was still moving. I looked closer at him and recognized the tic-like twitch near his mouth that I had seen in some of the kids at the centre.

"This is Ms. Johnson's son. You know, the one who shared the camping slides," Erica said.

"Oh right! I really enjoyed her presentation," I said in his direc-tion. "What are you listening to?" I asked to confirm a theory I had.

"Nothing right now." He shrugged.

I smiled at him thinking that the untrained eye would assume that he was rapping along to a hip-hop song. It was probably his mum's idea to mask his tics. An adaptation technique to protect him from being a spectacle.

We went back to the second half of the program and heard a few more lectures from people who were running disability programs in Nigeria as well as experts from abroad.

"Just before I left to go to school in Michigan, I was in a pread-mission lecture in UNILAG," started a middle-aged woman dressed in colourful Ankara dress and head tie. "Suddenly a young lady who was walking down the steps to find a seat stopped in her tracks and looked like she was about to fall. Out of nowhere someone swooped right in and caught her, guiding her shaking body to the floor. Her muscles spasmed violently, and some other students sprang into action. They pried her mouth open and shoved a notebook between her teeth while someone fanned her and asked to give her some space. After some long suspenseful minutes, her body relaxed, and they gave her a drink of water. Then they got someone who knew her to help her get home. I was fascinated by the swiftness of those students who stepped in to assist her. They knew exactly what to do! They were aware. That is not to be taken for granted." She paused and scanned the room. "People in Nigeria are more familiar with epilepsy than they are with autism. They know that epilepsy is a disability . . . well, at least for those who aren't thinking the person is an *ogbanje*." Laughter erupted in the audience.

"Autism, like epilepsy, can also be managed. Ladies and gentlemen, even a little bit of awareness is powerful. It goes a long way. They say knowledge is power. That power can manifest even in the smallest, most intimate ways. See, ehn, we Nigerians are a stubborn people oo, let's tell ourselves the truth"—there were scattered chuckles in the audience—"but we are loving and helpful." She smiled and looked around the room.

"One of the things I missed about home when I moved to the States was how annoyingly helpful people here can be. Let's help one another. This is our collective burden. Ours is a society where training a child is a group responsibility. The village that it takes to train a child must consequently be trained to help that child in his or her vulnerable moments. I hope that this seminar will be one way of doing that. Thank you."

When the last presentation was done, there were three hours left for consultation. We moved outside to a small field where tents were set up for the therapists to do their assessments. Each tent was labelled with the specialty of the therapist, and the clients would be directed from one to the other for diagnosis and follow-up recommendations. I sat in the tent with Ms. Taylor, who was an applied behaviour analyst, and watched as she used play therapy and other techniques to assess functioning. The air buzzed with voices of different pitches as people who were already registered filtered through the tents.

Chapter 15

DISENCHANTED

About two hours in, a woman peeked into our tent looking like she was about to break down in tears as she prompted the young boy on her arm to come along. I recognized the woman from the mall. It was Midowa's neighbour. I greeted them and motioned them to their seats. The boy's name was Doyin. He did not speak at first but occasionally pointed and made sounds that were similar to the names of the objects he was indicating. Ms. Taylor explained to his mother that she would ask her some questions about her son's history and then observe his performance with tasks. I followed along in my checklist as the woman answered questions about his attention span, diet, and self-stimulatory behaviours. I then watched as Ms. Taylor switched from coloured blocks to numbered cards and instructed the eleven-year-old boy to arrange them in a certain order. His eyes darted around the room until he fixated on the charms on her bracelet and started to flick them. His mother repeated the instructions to him and guided his hands back to the objects in front of him.

"Does he have any trouble with school?" Ms. Taylor asked the boy's mother.

"Eeem, in his class his teacher is always complaining. In fact, sometimes he disturbs so much that they will keep him at the back because of others." Her voice shook as she squeezed the boy's arm, encouraging him to get back to the task. She looked to be in her late thirties, but the heavy bags under her eyes aged her. Her speech indicated that she had just a basic education, but her son went to one of the better schools.

"You're doing well, ma. He just needs someone to guide him. Don't worry, he will get it." I felt the need to commend her as I watched her shoulders drop in defeat. We continued to monitor the boy's responses and made notes.

"Ma'am, have you noticed that your son responds in distress to high-pitched sounds?" Ms. Taylor asked her.

"Yes, ma, especially in school. He doesn't like the bell at all."

Ms. Taylor nodded and watched the boy closely before scribbling on her notepad.

"According to my observation, Doyin meets the criteria for autism spectrum disorder. Please follow up with the Axiom Speech and Life Skills Centre." She handed her a referral note. "They have specialists there who can confirm the diagnosis and provide follow-up recommendations for you. Do you have any questions for me, Mrs. Ladoke?" She eyed the woman, who hesitated to speak.

After a long pause of deliberation, she raised her eyes from her son, and they gave way to a flood of eager tears.

"Ma . . ." Her voice broke and she swallowed. "I have taken this boy to churches, pastors, healers—there is nowhere I haven't gone. My friend took me to Odo Ajasa, a very far place." She snapped her fingers. "We met the priest in the river, and he was screaming at my son and ringing his bell, but the boy was just suffering." She started heaving and shaking her head. I felt a lump in my throat seeing the woman's agony. I pictured the scene just as it would be portrayed in Nollywood movies:

The priest and his attendants hover over the boy, who is kneeling in the shallow river purported to cure those possessed by evil spirits. He viciously grabs the boy and orders his attendants to fetch his giant bell. "Ah iro, you will hear me. Wa ri, the power of the master of the universe." His eyes blaze as he yells at the evening sky.

The boy shakes his hands free from the priest and covers his ears to protect his overstimulated brain. The attendants pull the boy's hands away so that the evil spirit will hear the rebuke.

The boy's mother stands aside, throwing some of the miracle water on her face as it mingles with the tears she sheds from seeing her son's small body writhing beneath the heavy weight of the men.

The neighbour friend who brought her to this place snaps her fingers rhythmically, thrusting her head from left to right and muttering incoherent words.

Really, what was a mother to do in such a desperate situation?

My mother would have done the same thing. Except that bell would have landed on the priest's head.

"Ma'am, you'll learn more about the risks of exposing him to such traumatizing practices at healing centres." Ms Taylor's voice brought me back to the room.

"I didn't know. I didn't know," the woman repeatedly cried, wiping her face and rubbing her son's head. I patted her back, assuring her that if she worked with the professionals, she would see improvements in time.

Midowa and I left the event around 6:30 p.m., as the organizers finished clearing out. I took off my heels, as my calves were tingling and throbbing. The long hours of hearing the endless tragedies of parents battling with their children's behavioural issues left me physically and emotionally exhausted. I told Midowa about the woman and her son, and he chimed in that she seemed to have been carrying the full weight of her son's disability, independent of her husband.

"I'm glad she was able to come and you guys helped her. That's the problem with this country. We think everything is about deliverance. So she was actually making matters worse by taking him to pastors?"

"Ehen, now as they will be shouting and ringing bell on the poor boy's head. Please, I need to buy something to eat before I faint." I had eaten during the break, but the day's activity left a gaping hole in my stomach. My options in traffic were limitless, and I still was not over the novelty of eating things that I had missed for years. I bought gala sausages, a bottle of Sprite, and oranges. It amazed me how you could eat a whole meal in Lagos traffic. Want eggs? Cake? Fruit? A dining set? You could get it all.

I looked the orange over, thinking it was peeled just right, not the way people just tear into it in America. I remembered how I would watch Muhmee peel an orange, the beautiful motion of her deft hands working around the fruit in perfect perimeter. The carve lines on a well-peeled orange were an art of their own. Starting at the top, my mother's knife would take off the peel, careful to caress the skin while leaving behind the tracks of her work. Experts like Muhmee would peel without wounding the white skin of the orange while novices like me would leave it looking massacred.

"There's no medical test for autism, unfortunately. It's just observation to see if the person fits the DSM criteria," I added to the conversation, ripping open the gala packet.

"So all the people who met the criteria had different symptoms?"

"Yeah, they were all different. I told you how the spectrum goes from mild to severe, so some people just had a few problems and others were more significant." We drove past a shop in Lagos Island, and I froze as memories flooded my brain. I knew the owner of that shop. I had been there many times with Muhmee before we left Nigeria.

Think, think about it.

Think about what, please? It was nothing.

Oh, was it really? The way he seemed to transform when he looked at her. The high-pitched voice that Muhmee adopted in his presence. That annoyingly placating way she said "hein," with a frozen smile on her face as she studied the man's wife when she wasn't looking.

"Hmm, so what's next?" Midowa's voice brought me back to the conversation. I opened my mouth to respond, my eyes coming back to focus as I oriented myself.

"Um, yeah. We referred them to centres where they have specialists who can start therapy with them. I wonder how many of them will actually follow up and what the outcomes will be," I said, suddenly feeling like I needed to run.

"Sounds like research for you, Madam Efiko. Hmm, na wa o. I hope our children won't have autism, abeg."

I stared at the orange, thinking how Muhmee was the only person I knew who would leave a whole string of peel from one orange. No breaks. It took discipline to do that, a kind of discipline that seemed to elude her when she did what she did.

"Our children," I heard myself repeat as my brain struggled to catch up to Midowa's words.

"Ehen, now, when we get married." He put his arm on my leg, tapping it lightly. I felt my muscles tense and the hairs on my arm stand up.

I sighed deeply, watching the traffic to gauge if we would be stuck in the car together all night. I wanted space between us and dreaded another robbery incident.

"Midowa, I think we need to talk," I blurted out before I was even ready.

"Sure, baby. What's wrong?" He grasped my thigh even tighter, and I heard my stomach grumble.

"Do you really see us getting married?" I shifted to face him. I was uncomfortable but felt it was the grown-up thing to do.

"Don't you?" he answered.

"So what's the plan if we do? Am I moving here, or are you coming to the States?" I raised my eyebrows in defiance.

He sighed, and I caught his eyes moving over the traffic.

"I thought this trip would help you want to move back. It looks like you have work to do here. I've been listening to all these ideas you're bringing up, and I can see it really concerns you."

"It's not that simple, Midowa." I purposely said his name sternly. "I have a whole life in America. Can you even imagine what it would be like for me to settle back here?"

"I know it won't be easy, but you're passionate about your work, and you'll do great things here. See, that boy now with his mum, you can really help them."

"And I intend to help, but I don't have to-to-to uproot my whole life to do that." I was stuttering like my mother.

"Why are you sounding so defensive all of a sudden?" He made sure to catch my eye.

"Midowa, we've already talked about this, and it's not fair to just leave this up to me to move back here. Do you know how hard it has been for me to adjust even on this trip?"

"Is it because of that robbery?" His voice suddenly dropped.

"It's not just that." I shifted back to move my body away from him. "You won't understand because it favours you. Do you know how many things I-I-I left hanging?"

"I'm not asking you to just leave all those things and come back. It will still take time, but I'm ready to wait as long as I have to," he insisted.

"That's not realistic, Midowa. I think we've both waited long enough. What-what-what are we doing here?"

He was tapping the steering wheel. Pushing up his glasses at intervals.

"What if I come over?" he asked. In all the times we had had the conversation, he hardly ever offered that alternative, and I analysed all the reasons why he may not be confident about that option. He was from a middle-class family, and understanding the sacrificing spirit of Nigerians, I knew his parents would give everything to support him financially for the move. I also knew well enough how hard it was to get visas in Nigeria, but it irritated me that he had never even tried. How easily he expected me to be the one to make it happen.

"That would be a different conversation, for sure. To be honest, that would make the most sense. I'm the one who has not even had any other relationship since I moved, so obviously I'm serious about this."

"Fair enough." His breathing slowed. "Hmm."

I wanted to say something but held back, as I felt my stomach churning and knew that I would need to get to a bathroom quickly.

"So are we breaking up?" he asked after a long pause. I resented him for asking that, again leaving me to do the heavy lifting.

"Yes," I said defiantly. "There's no point in stringing each other along. We can pick back up when you move."

He was right about one thing, I definitely saw there was work to be done, and I wanted to help as much as I could. I kept thinking about Mrs. Ladoke, who was isolated in her home by her husband and isolated in society and who constantly felt judged whenever she went out in public. There would be many more women like her feeling as if no one understood their pain, unaware that they are not alone. I wondered what it would take to set up support groups for them or at least a forum where they could meet to share space and encouragement.

But what stood out in my mind—what made it clear that this trip was well timed—was running into Osaruwa. We had a nice chat after the program and exchanged contact information. I was thankful that I found the humility to admit what I had done wrong and the bravery to make amends. I had looked forward to telling Midowa about it, but the current mood was not conducive to that conversation.

Midowa continued tapping the steering wheel, loudly, it seemed, despite the radio. For the first time, I became aware of how dreadfully long Lagos traffic can be. I shifted constantly, wanting to occupy the silence. Every so often I heard him draw a breath, and

I looked in his direction. He just kept looking forward, his eyes piercing through his glasses.

This boy is cold o, I thought. The Midowa I thought I knew would have begged me in that moment, made jokes, or at least started a random conversation to diffuse the moment.

This silence was foreign to me, and it felt dangerous. Did I ever really know him?

After the longest nail-biting hours in traffic, the car stopped in front of the building gate. I shifted to face Midowa and say an awkward good night, but he turned away from me and opened the door.

Relieved to see that he was coming around, I got of the car. He drew close, his tall frame towering over me.

"Mira." His voice was soft. He hadn't called me that in a while. My head hovered on his plain black shirt, not wanting him to see my eyes. It was a nice shirt, accentuated by his carved, broad chest. I was impressed by the fact that he kept up his physique this whole time and marvelled at the power in those muscles that hugged me so tight.

"Is this about your genotype?" he asked, rubbing my arms.

"What?" I squinted in the dark, genuinely confused.

"Are you AS? Is that why you're breaking up with me?"

"No." I scoffed. I was almost annoyed but actually felt sorry for him.

"So you checked?" he asked before I could say anything.

"No, I didn't have time, but I'm sure I'm AA."

He looked right at me, his eyes searching mine.

His hands fell to his sides. "Were you even worried that I was spending time with your friend?"

"What does that have to do with anything?"

"A girl who wants a guy for herself will not just send her friend to be spending time with her guy, and she's not a bad-looking girl."

"Okay, why does everybody keep saying that?" I muttered under my breath. "Maybe it's just me, but I believed you people are not animals. Trust, that's what it is. I'm not stupid. You both are people I trust, and if I can't have that, then please, why are we even having this conversation?" I tried to push past him and walk away. He grabbed my hand and pulled me back.

"I'm just trying to understand where this is coming from." He scratched his head and rubbed it.

I slung my bag firmly on my shoulders and held his arms.

"Midowa, I've been saying this since, you've just refused to face it. You know I'm right. We have to get serious about this now. You said it yourself that I might resent you if I moved back to Nigeria and became frustrated. I'm afraid that will happen, and I don't want it to. Let's act like adults and do the right thing here. In five years we may be married, talking about this moment and how things all worked out. But we have to be realistic now, and I'm telling you, Midowa, if you want me, then fight for me. Prove it by doing the work." I knew that my neck was rolling and that my American accent was on full blast.

He sighed deeply. "I will. I promise. I'm just worried that you'll forget me."

I scoffed. "I'm not the one who dated someone else."

The words fell out of my mouth before I could catch them.

"Come on, Samira. Really? You're just afraid of relationships. I mean, let's be real." He threw his hands up in the air.

"Midowa, please. Let's talk about this tomorrow. My aunty will be wondering why I'm not in yet. It's almost ten o'clock."

He hesitated and then said, "I'm sorry."

"No need to apologize. Good night." I half hugged him and walked through the gate, feeling his desperate eyes on my back.

The thing about life is that we are all going our own way, on a unique journey in a collective existence where our actions and inactions connect in a nexus that invariably weaves us to an end, some tragic, some benevolent.

When Midowa passed by that woman's store, he opened up a years-long injury that spewed malignant pus all over his good intentions. If we had not passed that store at that particular moment, perhaps I would not have had the courage to do what needed to be done and break free from a non-progressive relationship.

That store was owned by a woman I knew as Mrs. Godwin. She was married to our family doctor, who was always nice to us and sometimes dropped off groceries. His wife owned a jewellery store just outside Lagos Island, and although the shop always seemed to pull in customers, I couldn't understand why Muhmee took me there often. Mrs. Godwin was light skinned and believed to be pretty. She carried herself like a typical thick madam, and as I came to find out, she seemed even heavier anytime Muhmee was around.

On that night of the bike incident, we were actually on our way back from visiting the Godwins when that crazy man threw glass at me.

How wonderfully ironic.

I had left the Godwins' house full of malice and hatred for all adults in the world. They were liars, and they were disgusting. Perhaps that bike man was punishing me for such a vile thought.

At the Godwins' house, I had asked for the bathroom as the adults yakked about the involved oddities of their lives. It was a nice house; evidently, Dr. Godwin was comfortable in his upper middle-class station. From the bathroom, I heard Mrs. Godwin's laughter, like it was running on low reserve. I always felt like she was forcing niceties when we visited her shop and wondered why Muhmee didn't pick up on it.

When I turned on the tap to wash my hands, I noticed a poster on the wall advertising the doctor's hospital. It seemed vain to have such a poster in your own home, but I concluded that it was prudent for the visitors' toilet. *My father is a big shot in America*, I thought, deciding that I was not at all impressed. I stopped short at the bottom of the page where a set of phone numbers jumped out at me.

I felt like I had been punched in the gut, my throat suddenly seeming to close up.

08036048848

I felt the anger rising in my chest as it threatened to cave in and noticed the familiar taste of bile the first time I saw those messages on Muhmee's phone.

Messages from 08036048848.

You were looking so sweet today. I wish I could lick you like ice cream.

There were many more.

Why do I miss you so much like this? I just want to leave somebody in this house and run to you.

The sun doesn't set without reminding me that I need you in my life. Thank you for the woman you are. I wish things were different, but what choice do we have than to love with the heart?

I felt nauseated. The man couldn't even string together correct poetry, and why did he not even mention his wife by name. "Somebody" was what she was reduced to, a woman who is acclaimed in her shop quarters where young men would call out their wishes that they could marry her kind in their lifetime.

I never got to see Muhmee's responses, but entertaining those messages was equally criminal. I wanted my dad and wished that he didn't have to be gone for so long, missing out on key milestones in my life and risking being replaced by another man.

Until that moment in the bathroom, I had only suspected that Muhmee was having an affair, and I tried to distance myself from the thought. It all started one day when she asked me to get out a number for her from her phone as she talked to a neighbour. As I scrolled through the numbers, a text message came through, and the phone was on silent mode. I had caught the word *sweet* and hurriedly returned to the contacts to get the number. I thought about it all evening and decided to investigate. I managed to break into the phone very quickly when Muhmee was in the shower. I read the whole message and glanced at the number. It wasn't registered under any name. I had hoped that it was all a mistake and that some creep was stalking my mother with flirtatious texts. Then it became routine that I would sneak into her phone to read new texts. I only ever managed to see one reply from Muhmee: Hey God oo you're funny. The fact that there was an exchange and she hadn't saved the number was very suspicious to me. The verdict was in by the third time I read the messages: Muhmee was guilty of an affair.

I had started to recognize the number on Muhmee's phone but didn't know that I actually had it memorized until that day in the toilet. The recognition was unplanned and so damaging that I condemned myself for knowing such things that did not concern a thirteen-year-old child like me.

Midowa didn't know any of that, nor did he need to. The only person I had to discuss it with was Muhmee herself. At different points in my life, I had debated confronting her, to at least give her a chance to deny it.

What would Dahdee think of her if he knew? Would she even tell him? Should I?

I grappled with those questions for years but developed a mechanism of shoving them into the so-called Pandora's box until we drove past that shop. All that venom was eventually going to come bursting out. Breaking up with Midowa happened to be the most convenient outlet.

Chapter 16

BORROWED CONCLUSIONS

"You see, we were on our own o. Now the oyibo people have brought another problem for us again. Which one is autism?" I heard a man on the street lament as I marched with fifteen other volunteers to create awareness for autism. That was a common sentiment amongst many Nigerians—that the status quo is unpleasantly disturbed when such diagnoses start to creep into the vocabulary of the people. It is understood that by naming it, a new enemy has now been invited to live amongst them.

Two men playing draft in our outreach community summed up the word on the streets.

"Ah, madam. Make government first give us light and water before they will be looking for awetism, abi na wetin?"

"All the money they get in aide, nko. Do you know how much the UN gives Nigeria for humanitarian initiatives?"

"Abeg, leave those ones na to send us weapons and drugs so that we can finish ourselves, and they will now come and take away our resources!"

As I spent weeks working with Osaruwa and her team, I came to find that there were a good number of initiatives to normalize and fund programs for physical disabilities, which was a hard enough fight in a country that glorifies suffering and smiling. The fight to advocate for cognitive disabilities and mental health services on top of that was one that a few people were braving but coming up on pushback. The more I talked to people about why we were resistant to help, the more I realized it was a bigger issue than just not caring enough. Nigerians have learned not to depend on government programs because the government has its own burdens already and the economy needs saving. Really, who is going to dish out the funds to prioritize the taking care of such ones who were ill fated by some misfortune in life? That is a family matter, not a government matter.

I attended countless meetings with Osaruwa and learned more about the Nigerian spirit than I had ever known. I was both intimidated and encouraged by her response to the casual disinterest of government officials in our area of focus.

"Ahnahn, you ladies know we still have many of these community programs we are trying to sponsor. Ehmmm, look at this one—sickle cell. We just pumped millions into that one. So this, your autism, I don't know if it's really important."

Osaruwa had presented a sound argument to advocate for the program, and we still got rejected. We were aiming for success, and even our clothes had been well thought out. I had on a long bubu dress with a neatly tied headwrap, looking like a copy of my mother. Osaruwa too was dressed from head to toe in Ankara. Still, we were called small girls and interrogated about how many children we had.

Finally, we got an approval, just as I was preparing to return to the US. Osaruwa's perseverance and courage moved me to want to do more. If she and many others like her were so willing to make a difference with what little they had, how much more could I do with the ample resources in the States?

About a week before I was to return, I sent an email to Professor Bodorf, as promised.

Hello, sir,

I hope this email finds you and the family doing well. It has been an interesting time here in Nigeria. I wasn't aware that so much was being done with autism awareness and support programs for families. I have been working with some incredible people who have the resources and the right attitude to make a difference. So far we have obtained a grant to widen the scope of the outreach programs and provide more screening tools for children's centres. I was tasked to lead an initiative to start support groups for mothers whose kids have autism and increase their connection to the community.

My eyes have been opened to so many areas of opportunity, and I have narrowed down my master's interest. I plan to enroll at Pitt as soon as I return. I will be flying back to the US in two weeks and would love to process my time here with you.

Until then, stay well, and please give my love to your wife.

Regards,
Samira Ofunwa

As I spent time with Doyin and his mum, Mrs. Ladoke, I came to know the kind boy he was, in spite of his father treating him like a stranger while showering his siblings with affection. Along with Mrs. Ladoke, I recruited a group of mothers from the seminar to try out a peer support group. We agreed on a central location at a leisure centre, where the kids could play while the mothers processed their feelings. We cried collectively as the women shared their struggles, their husbands threatening to leave them, and their community shunning them. My last day with them was especially hard. I bawled as if all the tears I had accumulated were finding release.

I often questioned my decision to break if off with Midowa, wondering if it was impulsive. But there was an urgency that being in Lagos had imposed on me, like things needed to be done *shap shap*. I missed him, even though we had tried to maintain cordial contact. It felt unreal, trying to make conversation about everything but how much we missed each other. At times I wavered and almost asked him to forget everything I said. At other times I was too busy planning my next steps when I got back to the US.

This trip to Nigeria had changed something in me, the way I knew that it did in Nayana. I had newfound appreciation for how comfortable my life was and how that was holding me back. I kept in touch with Erica in Boston, and she promised to connect me with their research team for collaboration. I imagined how I was going to propose the research program to Ms. Rhonda for alternatives to restraints. I expected some pushback, with justifiable concerns for safety and reliability. But I was willing to compromise and consider any recommendations. I was done running.

The day I left Lagos, I had the worst stomach cramps ever. I couldn't tell if the bacteria-infected street food I had was punishing me or if it was just my nerves.

Midowa insisted on taking me to the airport, the one thing I was hoping to avoid. The conversation was not as painful as I had feared though. I had so much to tell him about my work with Osaruwa, and he was genuinely interested.

After my bags were checked in, I ran to the bathroom to empty my bowels, hoping that I could hold out on doing so again during the long plane ride to Amsterdam.

Midowa walked me to the security gate, and we faced each other to say goodbye.

"Samira, it's not like I just wanted you to move back all along. The visa situation in Nigeria has gotten so crazy—" Midowa started, visibly struggling to contain himself.

"I know. My friends have been telling me about it," I interjected.

He nodded with his eyes half-closed.

"It's just the fear that they won't give me one. Even people with better chances than me have been getting denied."

"But you have a good shot. Look at your job, and you're smart. You can come for your master's degree. My friend said student visas have the best chance."

"Yeah, so..." He was fingering a lump in his pocket.

"So." I adjusted my bag, shuffling my feet.

"Just be patient. I'm working on it." He pushed his glasses up, and his jaw tensed.

I nodded.

He hugged me tight for a long time.

"I'm not in a hurry to start anything new. Trust me, I have more important things to worry about." My voice had taken on an odd pitch.

"So you're going to start the research at work?" I caught a glint in his eye as he asked that, as if reassured that I would be busy with my work goals.

"Yeah. I've been emailing with Ms. Rhonda, I'm hoping to get paid while I do the research. Enough free work."

"Nice. That's really good," he whispered, looking down. "So no more midnight calls?"

I shook my head, trying to be coy. "But we can always gossip about things going on."

He reached into his pocket and pulled out the lump that was in decorative wrapping. He put it in my hand and closed my fingers over it.

I squeezed the package and felt a round shape. I ripped it open, seeing that people were filing in through security, and I was falling behind. I pulled open another transparent wrap and could see it was a silver charm bracelet. I took it out and examined the charms.

A heart, a butterfly, and a round plate. The inscription read *Midowa and Smallie Forever.*

"Awww, this is so sweet." I smiled at him, then looked back down at the bracelet.

"I had already gotten it before . . . you know. I didn't want you to have something from Tega and not from me," Midowa said, and in that moment all of my resolve not to cry almost broke.

I looked at his face, longing and vulnerable. I pulled him into a hug and sniffed hard, forcing the rogue tears back.

I returned the bracelet to its packaging and smiled. I picked up his hand and pressed the lump into it, closing it with both hands.

"This is so special . . ." My voice broke, and I blinked rapidly to clear my blurring vision. "Save it for me. Give it to me when you come the US. I want you to look at it as motivation and to know how wonderful it will be when I get it back." I held his gaze intently and watched his face fall.

"Save it for me," I repeated, touching his cheek as a tear finally fell on mine.

He pressed his lips together, nodding and adjusting his glasses.

"Okay," he croaked. "Okay."

"Okay," I said, pressing his hand. I wrapped my arms around his lower back, feeling like the floodgates of tears were about to burst all over him. He squeezed me, and I collapsed into him, inhaling the gorgeous scent he had worn to impress me.

I was aware of people around me, talking loudly and admonishing their loved ones with goodbye instructions. I pulled away and wiped my face.

I planted a kiss on his cheek and picked up my hand luggage.

"Safe trip," he called after me, still holding on to my hand.

"Don't lose my bracelet o!" I yelled to him before disappearing from view.

As the plane lifted off the tarmac, I looked out at the city of Lagos that had been home for the past five weeks. I sighted the city lights from traffic in the distance, wondering what madness those people would have to endure to get home that night.

Lagos, the centre of excellence. Yes, to live in that city, you had to excel in whatever you were doing, better if it was legit and even more excellent if it was not. Lagos taught me to take no prisoners—to take what's mine and to never take no for an answer. It was indeed a pacesetter of a city, notwithstanding the overflowing drainage systems and constant stench of sun-boiled urine.

I knew I would be back before long. As Osaruwa told me, "You have to stay and get used to it. Staying away will only make it worse."

I didn't know if Midowa and I would ever get back together. I suspected that when I returned to the comfort of my American life, the romance would return to me, and we would pick right up where we left off. There was no room for that romance in Lagos, no room for enchantment. You had to shine your eye at all times. In all the chaos of Lagos life, I acquired a new impatience for anything that did not fully serve my purpose.

Even as my stomach rumbled throughout the flight, I concluded that of all my life's adventures, none was as meaningful as my time in the city where people live on the edge of fear, unafraid.

Lagos.

EPILOGUE

"Hey, Dorcy, look at me. Do you like my earrings?" I finger my ears, drawing the boy's attention to the carved image of the African continent. I move closer to him, slowly. His hands are covering his ears as he screams at intervals. His eyes linger on my feet and occasionally lift towards my head.

One of the other kids had accidentally kicked his train set, and he got agitated.

"Derrick, stay!" I call to my colleague and nod at the other two to move the rest of kids out of the play area where Dorcy has scattered his toys in anger. They shuffle the children out as quietly as possible, and I thank God that they did not object. Derrick turns off the TV and closes the blinds, enough to dim the room while allowing some light.

"You're okay, buddy. I know you're frustrated, so frustrated," I assure him in a calm voice, inching closer while giving him some space. Derrick turns on the sound machine to a waterfall, which usually calms Dorcy. I make eye contact with Derrick, and he moves to a corner of the room, out of sight but present in case I need assistance.

Safety.

I run down the checklist of things the SONG de-escalation steps require. Looking around the room, I make sure there is no object that can cause harm. After a few minutes of letting the quiet ambience take effect, I raise my hands in the air and call out to him.

"Dorcy, what is this?" I make my voice more high pitched than usual. He doesn't look up at me but is shouting in a lower tone.

"Dorcyyy, what is this," I call again in a singsong voice, waving my hands in his line of sight until he finally looks up. "Dorcy morsey, what is this?" I wave my hands above my head in the silliest animated way I can manage.

Openly distract.

"Haafaaa," he croaks.

"I can't hear you, Dorcy. What is thiiiiisss?"

I move my right hand closer to his face, and he yells out, "Haafaa!"

"Yes, buddy. High five!" He slaps my palm with one hand, and I reach the other to touch his hand.

"Good job, buddy!" This has become a little game of ours, and we proudly added it to the vocabulary of new words he is starting to say.

Derrick pulls out a pressure blanket from a resource bin and stands ready for my cue. I do a few more high fives with Dorcy, and when he seems distracted enough, I signal to Derrick to bring it over. "I'm gonna put the blanket on you, okay, buddy?" I announce before throwing it over him.

Negotiate.

"Okay, buddy. Do you want to count some stars or show me your train set?" I repeat the question, as he seems distracted by my earrings. "Which one, buddy? Count the stars in the sky or the choo choo train?"

"Tarrrr," he mumbles.

Guide.

"Excellent choice, my friend." I sigh internally, thinking we could all use the calming ambience. I secure his blanket tightly in place and guide him towards his favourite beanbag sofa.

Derrick goes over to the night star lamp in the corner and turns it on. He shuts the blinds all the way as the green and violet stars dance across the ceiling. We both sit close to Dorcy as he stares up at the ceiling, humming in a low growl. I hear the other kids' voices carrying on with their night routine. I catch my breath, practicing my paced breathing to ease my anxious nerves.

The collaboration with the research team is starting to pay off. Just three days ago, I tried the SONG technique with Dorcy, and after multiple attempts, we eventually had to restrain him or risk someone getting hurt. It wasn't perfect, but with consistency and patience, there was hope that it would eliminate the need for physical restraints.

I have been back in the States for six months now, and the lessons I learned in Nigeria remain with me. I enrolled in the applied behaviour analyst program and was approved to start my research project at the Kerr centre. I was especially proud to tell Aunty Zubaida that I would finally be getting paid and for that reason would be moving in with her. She had all kinds of objections to that and still does when she comes home to our modest two-bedroom apartment.

Muhmee just asked me to accompany her to the mall to help her pick out some new shoes. She does not need me for that; she keeps finding excuses to hang out since I moved out of the house. When I came home from Nigeria, I wasn't sure how I could face her without blurting out my rebuke for her affair or just being weird. Then I returned to find that she had cooked my favourite dish. Despite her usual rant about random things that annoyed her, she had told everyone how much she missed me. I don't know if I'll ever ask her about the doctor. I just know that I would want it to be an adult conversation without any meltdowns. At least not on my end.

As for Midowa, he was admitted to a Texas business school. He says he's been working with a visa agency to start the application process. I praise his efforts and provide small doses of encouragement while maintaining cordial distance. As promising as that sounds, I can't guarantee anything. It could very well be that by the time he actually comes over, I will have moved on or just lost interest. I'm still like the madman running, just like the women in my family whose decisions have brought us all to this point in time.

I am not and probably will never be Dr. Phil. As Dahdee so wisely put it, I am just an insignificant stick bound with others to make one exacting broom. Together we are counted as a growing number of willing hearts, making a difference, stroke by stroke. We may not get every speck of dust in the house, but we will continue to sweep, one stroke at a time. And boy will we sweep!

THE END

www.ingramcontent.com/pod-product-compliance
Lightning Source LLC
Chambersburg PA
CBHW020143120726
47903CB00007B/2395